SHADOW
DANCERS

SHADOW

A Margaret K. McElderry Book

ATHENEUM   1983   NEW YORK

DANCERS

JANE LOUISE CURRY

For my brother Bill

———————————————————

Library of Congress Cataloging in Publication Data

Curry, Jane Louise.
Shadow dancers.
"A Margaret K. McElderry book."
"An Argo book."
Summary: Wrongfully accused of stealing a
valuable moonstone, Lek the conjuror determines
to enter the dread Shadowland where the sun never
shines and search for the long-sought Opal Mountains
where he might find another stone with equally
potent powers.
[1. Fantasy]   I. Title.
PZ7.C936Sh   1983   [Fic]   83–3733
ISBN 0–689–50276–1

Published simultaneously in Canada by McClelland & Stewart, Ltd.
Composition by Maryland Linotype Composition Co., Inc.,
Baltimore, Maryland
Manufactured by Fairfield Graphics, Fairfield, Pennsylvania
First Edition

Twelve circles spinning to the Oldest's will,
Twelve stars a-circling the Wheel-Star Lurizel,
Twelve stones a-sleeping under Timmerill Hill,
Twelve spheres a-rounding under Kyth's hands' skill.

Twelve stones a-shining in the dark stream's sand,
Twelve stars a-shimmering on the sky's dark strand,
Twelve shadows circling in a strange, dark land,
Twelve slaves a-dancing in the dark lord's hand.

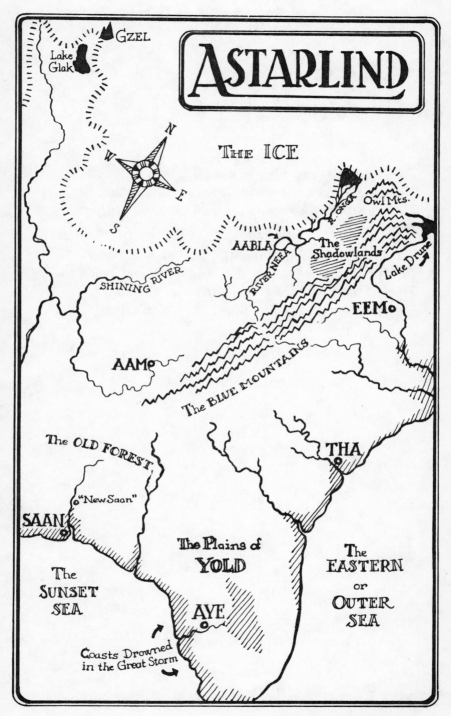

Map drawn by the author

CONTENTS

I. ASTARLIND

1. RIDDLE

FOR ALL HIS YEARS, the great raven's eye was as keen as
ever, or he would never have seen the Man. Perhaps now
he soared more and flapped less on a long journey than
he did in his youth in the days of the First Time, but that
was no wonder. He was Hlik, greatest of the Ravens of
Domgrath, on an urgent errand to the Wolves of Aam
from Basadil, king of the Deathless Folk. As the Ravens
called the Aldar, or elves; for though some among the
Ravens of Domgrath were as old in years, they were none-
theless mortal. Oldest of them all, Hlik was the largest of
his folk. He passed in size even the great snow owls, and
equaled the eagle in all but the spread of his dark wings.
Little escaped his eye.

Winging eastward out of the empty lands, Hlik spied
the western branch of the River Neea, and turned in a
wide, graceful curve to follow its line south. Below, his
shadow dipped and flashed across the treetops of the Forest of Aabla, the ancient wood that breasted the wide
river and stretched away for leagues until it met the swift
East Neea. Its bobble trees and lacewillows were winter-
bare, a gray haze of branch and twig clouding the first-
fallen snow, but the sight warmed his heart, for he had
been young there long ages past, a dweller on the great
river-bounded "island" of Aabla, in the city of Aab.

Aabla! Its city, once a place of white towers, of bowers and green gardens, was now all forest. The Forest had conquered the greatest of the cities of Astarlind when armies could not. It had been a wilderness for tens of centuries—since the end of the First Time, when Basadil, King of the Silvrin branch of the Aldar, led his folk out of Aabla into their mountain fastness of Avel Timrel.

Ahead, Hlik saw the first of Aabla's groves of malin trees and was half-tempted to drop down and glide among their golden leaves. Because these were not shed until spring, when the new buds swelled, even in winter the groves were a lovely echo of days when all the year was summer and Aab the loveliest of all the cities of the Aldar.

Hlik veered sharply when he saw the Man. Riding down the wind, he circled close above the treetops around a spot where trees had been felled to make a small clearing near to the river bank. The morning sun had melted the snow in patches, revealing in one place a shallow pit where an ancient pavement of colored stone had been uncovered. A little tent of skins was strung up between two trees. The Man, wrapped in a tattered blue cloak, with a grimy bandage tied around his head, knelt nearby. He appeared to be digging.

Strange, Hlik thought. Why should a mortal labor to uncover the old elvish works? Since the Times Before, Men had hated the Silvrin elves—or the memory of them, which came to the same thing. Of the three branches of the people of Aldar, only the Silvrin had crossed the Eastern Sea to Astarlind, and, being first-come, they judged all that land their own and all Men trespassers in it.

Unobserved, the great raven dropped down to perch high in a malin tree, all but one bright eye hidden among the golden leaves. He found himself mistaken. The Man did not dig to find more of a ruined house, but to fashion a burying hole. Beside him, the tiny figure of a lemmy lay

14

stretched out in death's awkward stiffness. At least, it *seemed* to be a lemmy. It was a small, wide-eyed, short-furred creature with slender limbs and a long, thin tail—but it was dressed in a short blue coat with a particolored hood!

The Man scrabbled in the earth with his hands and a bit of broken pot. When he had dug the hole deep and wide, he hugged the dead animal to him, weeping bitterly all the while. Then he laid it gently down in its earthen bed and covered it over and set to fetching stones to heap upon the grave. Carrying the last, heavier than the rest, he stumbled, staggered a little . . . and disappeared.

The man disappeared—and the rock he had held bobbed on across the clearing, to settle gently atop the mound of stones.

A moment later the Man reappeared, steadying himself with one hand upon the rockpile.

"Most curious!" thought Hlik as, with a lift of his great wings, he set out again on his southward way. "I must ask the Wolves of Aam what they know of this."

2. NORTHERN SNOWS

LEK THE CONJUROR, pressing doggedly northward through the snows of early winter in search of Uval Garath, the Opal Mountain, in company with the wolf Findral, had come at last to the furthermost foothills of the Blue Mountains. Below, Lake Drune lay like a dark scythe across their path. Two leagues beyond its frozen northern shallows, the cliff face of the Great Ice stretched away east and west, a gleaming line dividing the white sky from the white land.

Lek shaded his eyes with a fur-gloved hand and peered northeastward, straining to pierce that white glare.

"See there—smoke!" exclaimed Findral. "There, to the right of the cleft in the Ice. It seems the Icelings were right."

Lek, whose eyes were not so sharp as those of a Wolf of Aam, spied first one pale gray-white plume of smoke and then its neighbors. There were five, one for each of the five great fire mountains of the Ice, Mount Kadah and her sisters. Lek sighed.

"I had hoped . . ."

There was no need to say more. Two weeks earlier, in a chance encounter with two giant Icelings, Findral had seen his companion's quickly masked distress at the news of great eruptions in the fire mountains whose sharp peaks jutted up like dark islands on the ice sheet. In the Times Before they had towered over a green and hilly country, but even in those days the fires of Uval Garath—the legendary Opal Mountain that Lek sought—had long been dead.

"There are the Owl Mountains, somewhere to the west. We might look there," Findral said reluctantly. He had never seen them, but their dark slopes and passes were said to be perilous for travelers, beast or Man.

Lek turned swiftly. " 'Somewhere'? Where?"

On the third day of Zillimoon—the third day of the new year—Man and Wolf reached dark Drune's northernmost inlet. Between it and the Ice stretched wide, snowy barrens. Lek unslung and strapped on his Iceling snowshoes and quickly fell into a swinging gait that was almost a match for Findral's lope.

After two days they climbed onto a high and rolling plateau that in fairer weather would have been grasslands grazed by reindeer and oorus. Now the only tracks in the snow were of a small herd of ammuts, great, shambling beasts too large for an Iceling to hunt, let alone a solitary man, and too thick-skinned for a full wolf-pack to harry even if they dared. But Findral had a knack for catching snowcocks where those birds had burrowed into drifts for warmth, and so the companions dined well. On the twelfth day past Midwinter they came to the sparse, wind-bent fringes of a woodland that stretched for many leagues: all birches. The Silverwoods, Findral guessed. Away from the wind off the rolling plain, the birches grew taller and more thickly—slender, silver barked and lovely even in their winter nakedness.

Still keeping to their westward way, Lek and Findral made great speed, but even after four days saw no end to the forest. One league, one furlong even, looked—trunk and branch and trackless snow—exactly like the one before, until at last it came to seem as if, dream-fashion, the forest kept pace beside them. As if, while they slept in the moon's dark hours, the birchwood rustled on ahead to wait them on the morrow.

But on the fifth day in the wood, at noon, they were wakened from this foresty daze by a loud, harsh call.

"*Pru-uk-k!*"

A raven larger than any Lek had ever seen flapped down through the trees to perch on the lowest branch of a birch close by. He cocked a bright eye at the travelers. "At last! It has taken me weeks enough to find you."

"Hlik!" Findral cried joyfully, and capered around the tree trunk like a pup.

"*Pr-r-ruk!* Good meeting to you, young Findral. And this, I take it, is the conjuror the Wolves of Aam and the three young Tiddi rescued from the fortress of Gzel. I have heard the Icelings' tales of that adventure." The old bird gave a cackle of amusement. "*Pr-r-rak!* An age of the world has passed since your kinds went adventuring together. The sight of you makes me feel quite young again."

Findral sank back of his haunches, panting, and Lek unslung his pack and sat upon it. He shook his head wonderingly.

"Hlik of Domgrath! The Wolves said you still lived, but I scarce believed them. Astarlind is a strange land indeed. When I left Umeár I did not know that I was sailing into the legends of the Times Before."

"*Pru-uk*, and why not, when you came in search of a legend?" The old bird cocked his head, eyeing the Man as if he were taking the measure of a new and baffling creature. "And why do I find you here in the northern wastes? I have circled Eem all this week past in search of you. I supposed that wisdom and weather would have sent you down out of the Blue Mountains into Eem's kinder snows

until the spring. Then, on my way north to Norn to ask if
the Icelings had news of you, I spied your tracks beside
Lake Drune. Madness! In all of Astarlind only the Shadowlands are more bitter in Midwinter than the shores of
Drune. Have you given up your quest, Conjuror, that you
leave the Blues at your back?"

A frown shadowed Lek's eyes. "Uval Garath, the Opal
Mountain, does not lie along the ridges of the Blues. I
have seen enough of them to be sure of that. Their long,
sharp-toothed ridges march along together from the Hazy
Pass east of Aam to their foothills at Drune's edge. But
Uval Garath stands on its own. Or so at least said my
Master Azra's oldest book of lore. Uval Garath was a fire-
mountain so old that its fires went out when the world
was still half-shaped."

He turned on Hlik a gaze half respectful, half sus-
picious. "If the Ravens of Domgrath are as old as the
legends tell, it is curious that you do not know where the
Opal Mountain lies. It is said that though the mountain
Uval Garath and the city of Avel Timrel were lost to Men
in the Second Time, still they were not utterly lost, but
only hidden."

"*C-rr-rk!*" Hlik nodded consideringly. "But much has
changed since the world and I were young. Aabla and
Aam still lie where they did in the First Time, but new
mountains have been lifted up and others thrown down. If
Uval Garath is still in the world, in this Third Time, then
it is well hidden."

The raven's look was hooded, but Lek did not notice.
His fierce, gray gaze searched the far horizon. "It still
exists. It must! I have seen it many times in a dream of
foretelling: of the mountain, and great opals gleaming in
its veins, and my hand reaching out to cup a glinting, blue-
green globe that wanted only polishing to make it another
Nirim, a second Worldstone for the King of Umeár."

"A foretale? Or a wish? And if you found such a stone, what then?"

"Why, then, sail home to place it in the King's hands as I was to have done fourteen years ago, before it vanished and I was named its thief. I would be Kell again, not Lek the outcast, conjuring for silver pennies. Kell! Master in my dead Master's house in Gellin." His eyes were bleak.

"Is that all you would do?" Findral asked. "What of the Tiddi? What of Arl's Stone, Mirelidar? And of the Naghar, with all his Men and goblins, who claims that Stone for his own?" These were questions he dreaded asking, for though there was much in the Man to love—courage, strength and ready wit—there seemed little warmth or affection. The young Wolf feared that Lek might one day shrug off such friendship as his and that of the Tiddi Arl as easily as a cloak. And yet—it was no wonder that his thoughts should turn always to the lost Worldstone, for it was one of the Twelve, and a treasure beyond price.

From a patchwork of old Tales and the teachings of his old Master, the Wizard Azra, Lek had gleaned something of the history of the Twelve Stones. In the dawn of the First Time they were mined in Uval Garath and shaped for the Great Dance by Kyth the Maker. Made in the image of—and sharing the powers of—the Nine Planets and the Sun and Moon and Wheel-Star, they were entrusted to the twelve elven princes of the Aldar, to be taken each Midwinter to the Isle of Thamor and the Great Dance. There, twelve dancers carried the magical Sky-stones in the yearly celebration of the Sun's First Rising. When at the end of the Second Time Lisar the Sunstone was stolen, the Sun itself dimmed, winters deepened, and the Ice crept down from the North. So had the loss of Nirim darkened Lek's life and chilled his heart.

"What of the Tiddi?" Lek shrugged. "The Tiddi are a little folk and good at keeping to themselves. They will fare well enough if they stay clear of Aam and Eem and all between. We have seen no enemies these three months past. Who knows? Perhaps the Lord Naghar's Men or his goblins—the Rokarrhuk, as you call them—fled Astarlind at the news of the fall of their citadel at Gzel. These things are no concern of mine. Astarlind is a fair land, but not my own."

"Spoken like a Man," croaked Hlik drily. "But tell me, Conjuror, why do you follow the old way west to the River Neea and Aabla? Are you to meet someone there, perhaps?"

Lek looked at him blankly. "I know nothing of Aabla, or where it lies. We mean to look for Uval Garath among the Owl Mountains. Findral says that they lie another day's march ahead, on our right hand."

"Indeed." Hlik ruffled up his neck feathers. "Their foothills step down to the old road's side. But you will find no fire mountains among the Owls, dead or live or sleeping. They are deep, rumpled hills, thick-clad with stunted pines, and where they stand there stood in the Times Before only a high, upland plain."

"The stars be praised!" Lek said in a bitter, mocking voice. "My fortunes never change. So where must I search now? The far Indigoes, or the Dragon's Teeth, the mountains that edge the Outer Sea beyond?"

"No!" Findral, for his part, was much cheered. He had not looked forward to braving the Owls, for they were well named, and the owls who guarded them were said to be as large as forest wolves. The Wolves of Aam were larger, but against a winged creature that might be no great advantage. "No, we shall seek out the Lost City of Avel Timrel and the magician you once spoke of—the Wizard Orrin. He will know where Uval Garath lies. You have said so."

His eagerness brought back Lek's smile. "I have hoped

so, let us say. Yet I fear I shall still be searching when I am white haired and shamble footed. The Lost City is not meant to be found by Men."

"*R-r-rk!* But the Wolves of Aam once knew it well," Hlik said slowly, as if he took care to be neither encouraging or disheartening.

"And I shall know the road there if I see it," said Findral with a wolvish grin. He cut a caper in the snow. Finding Avel Timrel was a quest more to his heart's liking than the search for Uval Garath. Only a Man with an axe to grind would prefer a mountain honeycombed with old mines to one that hid the splendors of Avel Timrel, the Lost City of the Silvrin. "It lies deep within a wilderness of mountains, surrounded by the Fennethelen, a passless ring of peaks crossed only by the Wolf Way, a narrow paw's span wide. '*A Way but no pass, Over peaks of black glass,*' the old Song says."

Findral's dreaming look faded, and he drew a deep breath. "But we must find it before the end of springtime, when I must return to my own folk. What news, Great Hlik, do you have of the Wolves of Aam?"

The raven settled himself more comfortably upon his bough. "I was with them early in Morimoon, so the news is over two months old, but your mother Renga bade me tell you three things. First, the Moonstone Mirelidar came safely to Werrick on the Deep Ice, where it lies in a guarded vault beneath the Icelings' buried lodge. Secondly, that since the destruction of the fortress of Gzel a new danger has arisen. Men coming out of the Outer Sea and across the Farther West to swell the ranks of the Captain of Gzel now wander leaderless, roving in small bands, laying the land waste with careless fire and wanton slaughter of beasts. Do not run afoul of them. Some are simple Wild Men, but even they are not always to be trusted in these times."

"And thirdly?" Lek prompted. "The Rokarrhuk—the goblins—are they abroad too?"

"I do not think so. A company of them came out of the Blue Mountains through Eem to Tha in the month Nirimoon, but your friends Arl and Cat and Fith had brought warning in time to their Tiddi queen. The little folk disappeared like smoke before the wind—south to Aye, most likely. After a fruitless search the Rokarrhuk turned back, and none have seen them since. No, the 'Thirdly' was only a curious tale. At about that same time in Nirimoon the Wolves scattered a party of Men traveling in great haste westward near the headwaters of the Shining River, and freed an injured Man they held captive. But in the very moment that they loosed his bonds, *pruk!* He vanished."

"Vanished? In truth?" Lek stood up, knocking over his pack in his surprise.

Hlik gave a solemn nod. "In open country at noonday."

"Orrin the Wizard! It must be!" Lek exclaimed. "Why, this is the best of news. If anyone knows the road to Uval Garath, it will be Orrin." Hastily he retrieved his pack and thrust his arms through the carrying straps.

"Perhaps it was he. Perhaps," Hlik said, a little dampingly. "I believe that I saw the same Man not long after the Wolves' encounter, but before I heard their tales of it—a dark-haired, springy-legged Man with a bandaged crown, in a tattered blue cloak. One moment he was fetching a stone to set atop a cairn, and the next—Zzzt! Like a candle flame suddenly blown out, he was gone. The stone appeared to move across the clearing by itself, to settle atop the cairn. A moment later the Man was there again, dithering about like a feeble-minded ancient."

Lek frowned. "And he was not? Ancient?"

"Not he. His actions *seemed* those of an ancient."

Lek grimaced in disappointment. "Then it cannot have been Orrin the Wizard. Some lesser magician, perhaps, or a conjuror deeper in skill than I. But not Orrin the Enchanter. Orrin is old, perhaps the oldest of Men. He sailed west from Umeár in my grandfather's day."

"Still," Findral said hopefully, "we could travel west to Aabla to see spring in. It would do no harm to have a look at this vanisher."

"Nor much good," Lek said, but he smiled. "If you are so greedy to see deeds of magic, why—here!" He pulled off his left glove and with a conjuror's flourish drew out of the air a red rose that in that snowy wood blazed as if its petals were of flame. Findral watched wide-eyed until the rose glow faded to no more than a warm, sweet scent lingering on his friend's palm.

"Very pretty," said Hlik briskly. "But what am I to tell the Wolves? Will you make for Aabla or pursue the will-o'-the-wisp Lost City?"

"Better a will-o'-the-wisp than three months' waiting for the winter's end in the company of a crackbrained magician," said Lek. "But where . . ."

"Where indeed," said the old raven, not at all helpfully.

"'*West of the Blues, East of Aam*'," Findral quoted from the Wolves' song.

Hlik shrugged. "I wish you good fortune and kind weather, but I fear you will find only cold and hunger." With a beat of his great wings he lifted from the birch bough and soon was high above the trees.

"When you see the Wolves of Aam," Findral cried after him, "tell Renga to look for us along the Neea early in the spring!"

"'West of the Blues and East of Aam!'" Lek growled as, two days later, they climbed out of the Silverwoods onto a high, hummocky plain. They climbed slowly, for Lek's pack was heavy with game. The hunting had been good in the wood's western fringes. "Is that all your song says?

With such boundaries, Avel Timrel could be anywhere in a wilderness twenty thousand leagues square. It will take us more than three months to quarter so wide a land. What else lies within it?"

Findral considered. "The Rumples, a hilly country bordering the Neea. The deep gorge of the River Kithka. The Shadowlands. And many mountains and valleys our folk have not visited since the Times Before. I do not know their names."

"Shadowlands? The old raven spoke that name, but I took it for a figure of speech or a country of the mind."

"It is real enough, but no one travels there. Since the Coming of the Ice a great cloud has lain across it, even in the driest of Midsummers."

Lek's eyes narrowed. "A land of clouds? Such a land must have mountains to anchor its clouds, or the winds would sweep them clear."

Findral's heart sank, and with it his hopes of seeing the wonders of Avel Timrel. "It is an evil country. Who can say what holds the dark clouds there."

"Nonsense. High peaks, and a fire mountain's ash cloud, I'll wager. A fearful heart can make any shadow evil."

"The Wolves of Aam do not have fearful hearts," said Findral quietly. "Long ago, before the Shadow spread so wide, our folk hunted in its borderlands and told how even the hunted mousel turned away from that land, choosing the Wolf's tooth rather than going further into that shade."

"We shall see," Lek said vaguely. "Even if there are mountains, we can do no more than look at them, for their passes will be winterlocked, and willy-nilly we must go on to Aabla and return in spring." As they breasted the long hill, he turned with a laugh. "I know what ails you. You and your Avel Timrel. A Wolf in love with a fairy-tale palace!"

Findral paused on the snow hill's crest, but did not speak. Lek knelt to tighten the bindings on his snowshoes and looked around him. To the west across the rolling highlands nothing was to be seen but a sky clouding with the promise of snow. To the south, here and there a shaft of pale sunlight played across the rising, far-off hills, but beyond them a pall of darkness edged the sky.

"Another storm, and a fierce one! We will need to hurry to make much distance before it comes upon us."

"It will not come," Findral said. "In a thousand years it has grown, but never stirred. That is the land even Hlik fears, the land we call the Shadowlands."

3. UNDER THE SHADOW

IT WAS A GRIM LAND and grimly cold, yet under the Shadow the snows did not lie so deep as beyond its borders. Neither, though a gray twilight shrouded them, were the wrinkled highlands and their winding gullies muffled up in darkness as Findral had expected. He was a little cheered, for like the dusk at day's end in the outer world, this noonday dusk was wolf-light, the day's best for travel or the hunt.

Lek turned to speak and sprang back in alarm, his hand upon his sword's hilt. Looking for Findral's white shape, he saw instead a great, gray shadow of a beast, like one of the terrors of Gzel that walked still in his dreams—one of the Dread Ones.

It was an illusion of the Shadow and lasted only a moment—a moment in which rock and tree and friend alike grew into shapes darkly strange and threatening. But the beast had Findral's golden eyes, for the Shadow had not darkened them.

Lek drew a deep breath and shook his head in impatience at his own foolishness. Just as the Wolves of Aam were larger than forest wolves, so would Findral of Aam have been small beside the ancient Dread Ones. Only his color had changed now, darkening into an echo of the gray world just as it had paled from gold to white when first they set out across the snows, for such was the magic of the Wolves of Aam.

Seeing Findral's puzzlement, the conjuror made no explanation, but with an air of not caring in the least that they had left the Sun behind, sat down upon a boulder to loosen the lacings of his snowshoes. He was glad to shed them and sling them over his shoulder, for the pack that bulged under his cloak had made the swinging snowshoe lope more a hardship with every day that passed. The frozen meat he carried—peeka, snowcock, a reindeer haunch—was enough for two for a week in the deserted Shadowlands.

Findral, unburdened, ranged ahead, choosing a winding way southward along ice-clad streams that threaded a maze of deep hollows. Tattered clumps of frozen reeds rattled dismally in the chill wind, and the birches that had made the Silverwoods eerily winter-lovely were stunted here and clad in ice. Here and there firs huddled among them, unfriendly groves that even in a brighter land might hold dark dangers, a giant mountain bear or deadly hill-cat. In the Shadowlands no such beasts came hunting, but the dark groves threatened still, as if they might hold terrors nameless, and more dreadful.

Lek whistled softly, and Findral trotted back to his side. Lek pointed skyward. High above and perhaps four or five furlongs distant, a great bird soared on silent wings. A pale shadow on the gray sky, bending now this way and now that, it slid north along the hill that shouldered down to curb the frozen rivulet the travelers followed.

"A snow owl. And hunting," Findral observed softly. "Yet what meal can it hope to find? I've not seen as much as a snow hare's track. Unless—let us hope it has not caught wind of the meat you carry. Come!"

As the Wolf sprang for shelter Lek followed, half crawling, half sliding into an icy thicket as the white shadow slipped nearer, dropping below the hill's crest.

"An owl!" Lek marveled. "Its wingspan must outmatch even the great eagle's. I have never seen its like."

They watched uneasily until the great owl's flight lifted. Once above the hill's brow it wheeled and drifted westward out of sight.

"What *does* it hunt," Lek muttered, "when all there is to find is snow?"

"Excepting us," was Findral's soft reminder.

Imperceptibly the way among the hills led upward until, on the third day after they had ventured under the Shadow, Lek and Findral saw through a distant gap in the hills a shadowy line of hills higher still and climbed the rocky bluff that glowered over their streamside path, the better to see the way ahead. Some fifteen or twenty leagues distant, a line of tumbled slate-gray hills stepped down to meet the climbing highlands, and behind them loomed darker shadows still.

To the Wolf's eyes that Shadowland was as clear-edged as sunny midday to a Man. "There are mountains!" He danced a little in his excitement. "Dark and steep, and the shadows sit upon their crowns. Perhaps we have not come out of our way after all. But they are a long walk from here."

"We shall be hungry before we are out under the open sky again," Lek said, but his eyes shone as he spoke.

Findral grinned. "Not I. Wolves are not like Men, to be chained to mealtimes. One good feast from your pack, and I can go for nearly half a moon before I stumble."

"Excellent!" said Lek, with the first smile Findral had seen since they turned their backs on the open sky. "Feast, then. I shall go faster with a lighter load."

· · ·

They spied the campfires after nightfall.

"So no one travels underneath the Shadow!" came Lek's soft, accusing whisper.

Cautiously, Findral poked his nose out from behind the great boulder that sheltered them for a better look at the twinkling fires of the encampment halfway down the little V-shaped valley.

A confused clank and murmur, and now and then a shout, filtered up to them across the dusky snow.

"I make it ten fires," Findral murmured. "And they are not Men, only Rokarrhuk, the beasts that walk like Men."

Lek drew his breath in sharply. " 'Only'!" The memory of his prison in the fortress of Gzel—only three moons ago, though it seemed an age—made the word a snort half of excitement, half dismay. After a moment, he whispered softly, "Nagharot!"

It was Findral's turn to be surprised. "Nagharot? Here under the Shadow?"

"What better place for the Lord of these creatures to hide himself? The Captain of Gzel said that his Master's —the Lord Naghar's—realm lay eastward of Gzel."

"But half of Astarlind lies east of Gzel—or where Gzel was."

The conjuror could not see the great Wolf's grin at the memory of Gzel's destruction, but he heard it in his murmur. "Perhaps," Lek replied. "But where else could this Lord Naghar, as he calls himself, be free of spying eyes or curious passers-by?"

"As you say, perhaps," Findral said grudgingly. "If Rokarrhuk hearts are as tough as Rokarrhuk hides, they may have a bolt-hole here. But—a realm? Where brigand Men are bidden to share in war and plunder? We have traveled only ten leagues and are scarce beyond the borders of the Shadowlands, but already it weighs upon us. How long before this cold, dark dread would turn a Man's bones to water?"

It was true. The deathly stillness and dreadful sameness of the mazelike valleys were disheartening enough, but the deeper unease—the dark unfriendliness of hard, gray hills and bitter streams—must shadow the stoutest heart.

Lek gave a grim little laugh. "Ten days? You are right. Such a ragtag, outlaw army would melt away like snow in Mallimoon. But what of these Rokarrhuk? There are no such creatures in my homeland—unless they are the memory behind the Boggles that old wives on Umeár sing of to frighten naughty children: *His head be round to roll upon the ground, and his legs is bowed like a grandaddy toad. His nose be broad, his reach be wide. It do no good to run, it do no good to hide. He'll sniff you out from half a league away, and roll his noggin after you before you can say*

> *Hey, Boggle,*
> *Ho, Boggle,*
> *Roll the other way.*
>
> *I promise*
> *My Granny*
> *I'll be good all day.*"

Findral stared. "They roll their heads along the ground? I should like to see that!"

Lek laughed softly. Findral and his love for old tales and marvels! Though a brave beast and wilderness-wise, his heart was still a pup's. "What a gull you are! No beast alive can spare his head from his shoulders. It would seem you know as little of them as I do. Come, tell me: what can you spy of them from here?"

"Little enough. There are fifty, perhaps a few more,

perhaps less. One is taller than the others—a creature like your Captain of Gzel, I think."

"Fifty. Too many to be a patrol. What of their packs? How much do they carry?"

Findral shook his head. "They are all heaped together. I cannot—" He broke off suddenly. Lek saw his nose lift and his broad head turn as if he followed some movement across the sky.

"What is it?" he hissed.

Findral did not answer, but gave a warning shake of his head and crouched low, so that he seemed only another round, gray boulder on the rocky slope. Lek was no Wolf of Aam, able to take on the color of snow or stone, but he wore a white bearskin coat and boots of Iceling make. Shoving his gray cloak and heavy pack among the rocks, he stretched himself upon the snow, face down, his cheek cushioned on the fur that fringed his hood. He strained to hear, but there was only the crackle of harsh laughter far below. The cold he had not felt while on the move seeped into his bones and, impatient, he raised his head to chance an upward look. In that moment a wide shadow darker than the shadowed sky swept overhead and made a wheeling turn above the head of the valley, swooping down again across the boulders and the snowfield to the camp below.

"Another owl?"

Findral stood and shook himself. "A great Dusk Owl. From the Owl Mountains. It is strange to see one here— and keeping company with Rokarrhuk." He turned uneasily to scan the dark hills behind them.

Lek read his thought. "Yes. We should be higher up and better sheltered if these goblin folk have spies about."

They spent the night without a fire, in a tent of sorts fashioned from Lek's staff and cloak and ragged fur blanket. At dawn the fires far below winked out, and gray morning saw a heavy-laden Rokarrhuk column march swiftly out of sight. Following along the ridge top, at noon they saw the column reach the head of the next valley and climb into a rocky defile. They appeared once more, an antlike file cresting a far-off hill where a watery sunshine glinted on the snow.

"Northwest," Lek said.

"Yes, back to the Owl Mountains. And good riddance."

"Good riddance, indeed," the conjuror agreed. "If their Master is still after the Moonstone Mirelidar, the longer he thinks I fell at Gzel, the sounder I shall sleep. If he knew I searched for Uval Garath where the Twelve Star-stones of the Aldar were shaped, his owls would be hunting us in earnest. We must go warily."

They turned their backs upon the distant sunshine and retraced their steps.

4. ICE AND FIRE

FURTHER SOUTH, the stunted trees and scrub gave way to high tundra and sheer rock. When the day-long dusk deepened into night, the companions saw far ahead a faint orange-red glow, a tiny patch on the Shadow's hem that grew each night as they drew closer. Often even in the dark daytime they spied a far-off flicker on the underside of the heavy clouds.

With each day, too, their pace slowed, for their feet seemed as heavy as their hearts. Findral was the more fortunate, for the grayness of that land was not unpleasant to him. By day he scouted ahead through the wilderness of ash and stone and snow. Lek strode after. The pace was swift and steady, but not the long half-lope it had been. Lek's gaze was always seeking the high, barren heart of the far-off mountains. On the eighth morning Findral urged their turning back, but Lek's answer was to quarter the size of his own day's ration of frozen meat and return the rest to his pack.

"When we see the fire mountains I will turn back," Lek said. "Opals and old fire mountains go together. I promise that even if one among them sleeps, even if we see the mine workings, I shall come away content to return in the spring. But if you wish to go now, go. I will not hold you against your will."

Findral turned on him a look of reproach. Men had strange ideas of companionship if they took so little joy in it and gave so little trust. But then, no Wolf would be outcast from his kind for an unproven theft, as Findral knew Lek had been. Only for murder or madness would a wolf be cut off so cruelly. To be innocent, as Lek had been, and a child—the bitterness would be deep indeed. It would explain his dark moods and often distant manner. Strange that he, Findral, should be drawn to such a one. Man and Wolf, friends, when since the days of King Tion's grandson Arrn they had been enemies? But Findral put aside such dark musings and turned his mind to their trail. Such thoughts were the shadow of the Shadow, and dangerous to heed.

Lek saw resentment flare for a moment in the Wolf's eyes, like a sleeping coal that had been blown upon, and then die. Uneasiness darkened his mind, and it did little good to tell himself it was the Shadow's doing.

The weather worsened. Heavy snow squalls deepened drifts and masked treacherous, ice-glazed slopes and hid the mountains. Twice in the night ashes fell instead of snow, and they woke to a gray morning when the snow was darker than the sky. Their teeth gritted, and ash sifted from their coats as they walked. But on that day, the tenth under the Shadow, both silence and mistrust were broken.

After a nine-hours' wearying climb up a long, steep cleft, they discovered that they were among the peaks and had stumbled into a pass. They came out onto a high ledge overlooking a valley deeper and wider than any they had yet seen, its far wall steeper and higher than the ridge where they now stood. At their feet a narrow ledge ran steeply downward for about a furlong's distance. There a great rockfall barred the way. Its treacherous, icy rubble had to be tumbled off the ledge, and the travelers were a long while in gaining the windy valley floor. Once safely down, they did not rest, but fell into a loping run across the crusted snow to the frozen river winding down the wide valley. Findral did not slow his pace for the wind-scoured, rippled ice, and Lek was not far behind him, running with a light, sure stride.

When he came to where Findral waited under the steep cliffs, his eyes were hard as stars. "We are near. Very near. I feel it. Come! We have an hour—less perhaps—to find shelter before nightfall. This wind bites now, but by middlenight it will be bitter as a knife's edge."

They found a narrow, deep defile that might prove a stair to the cloudy regions among the peaks, but there was too little light left for exploring far. Nightfall brought a darkness so complete it seemed almost as if they were sealed within the rock itself.

When dawn's dusk reached in to touch their fur-blanketed huddle, the friends drew quickly apart and stretched legs and shoulders that were numbed and cramped with the cold. More often, now, the Shadow was in their eyes as they watched one another. Setting out, they found no sure sign that the broken cleft where they climbed had once been a travelers' way, but they kept on. Noon's rest they spent wedged for safety one above the other in a narrow rock chimney. In late afternoon they gained the shoulder of a high col above the head of the cleft and, looking down a steep and ashen snowfield, saw the line of an old track stretch down before them, an ancient shadow under the snow.

Away below, a valley far deeper than that from which they had climbed curved up from the south in a broad, steep-walled sweep eastward and south again. The mountains that echoed that curve were steep and sharp-peaked for the most part, but to the southeast three with broken crowns and thin plumes of ash and steam slumbered uneasily. From the summit farthest south, its crest all blown away, a thick pillar of gray rose to feed the clouded darkness that spread across the Shadowlands. It was a landscape out of a dark dream, stark and beautiful.

"The passless ring of peaks that guards Avel Timrel," Lek whispered. "The Fennethelen!" As much as Findral he marveled at their beclouded beauty.

"In the old tales all these mountains slept," said Findral with a wondering sigh. "And the sky was blue."

"In the old tales wizards and heroes came this way to Avel Timrel, not ragged conjurors and starving Wolves," Lek said wryly.

Findral stiffened suddenly, his ears pricking forward. "Ha! Perhaps not starving after all. Do you see? Below, across the valley, by that spur's foot. Either the snow moved, or a snow hare."

"Your eyes are sharper than mine," Lek said, and found himself speaking to the air as Findral, a gray wraith invisible against the ashen snow, sped downward.

Halfway, the Wolf stopped. When Lek caught up to him he was crouched in the lee of a wind-carved drift, his eyes fastened on the same point on the far side of the valley. Quickly, Lek knelt beside him. "What have you seen? Rokarrhuk?"

The valley floor appeared deserted, but as the conjuror strained to see, a faint movement—a stirring in the snowbank—caught his eye. Something burrowed there, but it was no snow hare scuttling out of sight.

A dark hole appeared. After a moment a small, pale face peered out and quickly disappeared. Then, to the astonishment of the watchers above, a small, thin, scantily-clad figure crept cautiously out on hands and knees and, with a nervous look this way and that, began to examine the snow, as if for tracks. After a last wary look up and down the valley he skittered back into his hole, to emerge a moment later with a bulging, patched skin sack. This he slung across his shoulders and set off in a crouching run across the valley bottom. As he toiled up the steep slope directly below them, Lek and Findral stared in disbelief.

A Tiddi? But all the Tiddi were a thousand safe leagues south, in Aye, or so Hlik had said!

Reaching a large outcrop of rock a furlong or so below the hidden watchers, the little creature passed out of their sight for several moments. Then they spied him again, clambering among the rocks. He stopped, dropped the sack he carried into a hole and, straining with all his small strength, tumbled five or six large stones—large, at least, for one so small—in on top of it.

"He has buried the sack," Lek murmured. "But why? And why is he here at all?"

The snow that had begun, unnoticed, to sift down through the grayness abruptly thickened, with here and there an angry swirl. "Hist! Look now," Findral said.

The little creature, a blur now, backed down the slope, taking care to step in his own footprints, brushing loose snow into each print as he went. The new-falling flakes quickly covered all trace of his going. The snowfall thinned briefly as he reached his hole across the valley, and Findral saw a little hand come poking out here and there, until the snow slumped down into the hole's mouth, to fill it.

Lek and Findral exchanged an unbelieving look. What was so spindly a little creature doing in so grim a place, in such grim weather? At first they had taken him for a Tiddi, but in fact he was too thin, too pale-skinned, too bent and crouching a little thing for a Tiddi. How could so frail a creature survive in a snowbank under the Shadow's frown?

In twenty minutes Findral was among the rocks,

sniffing out the buried sack. Lek shifted the little heap of stones.

"Well, here's another riddle for us," Lek said, sitting back upon his heels. The worn and much-mended sack—there was more mending to it than sack—held two much-patched but richly patterned fur cloaks and, jumbled all together, a few handfuls of shrivelled mushrooms and dried fish.

But they had no chance to ravel out the riddle, or even marvel more at it, for the ashy snow had turned to a gritty rain, and in the south, where the lowering clouds that cast the Shadow were the darkest, a great fiery rose bloomed and spread across the sky.

The world shuddered, and for a second's time all was silence. With the roar and wind that followed, coarse black ash lashed at them like some dark and stinging snow.

Man and Wolf shrank backward under the shelter of the outthrust rocks.

5. SEA-RISE

IN THAT SAME HOUR, some four hundred leagues to the south, Aye trembled too, if only faintly. There the setting Sun shone in a clear sky, but the grass mice came out of their holes to scurry aimlessly among the tussocks, and night birds—limpkins and night herons—deserted their perches to wheel blindly in the dazzling sky. The little horses in their pen nickered and milled anxiously about the gate, but because of the music and the dancing none of the Tiddi heard.

The Loorimoon feast began, as Tiddi moonfeasts must, at moonrise; and since the moon had risen in midafternoon, the celebration had begun then. All of the Tiddi, from little Minnow to old Skinner, joined Issa the Queen in dancing the Moon up. Afterwards came the feasting: plums and brambleberries, roasted gobbler and venison, sweet yumroots baked in their skins, persimmon bread and wine. Well before sunset contentment reigned, and the Song Circle beneath the ancient, spreading rockwood tree was ringed with small, dark, coppery bodies, sprawled or sitting cross-legged or, like little Minnow, curled in sleep like a fat-bellied wolf pup.

Old Singer, a small songbird in feather cloak and golden cap silhouetted against a cream and gold and rose-red sky, sat nodding in her willow traveling chair as Holly and Harr joined hands to dance Lis the Sun down, and Nee's flute sang Lis's last golden beam west away from the sea of grass, past the tree-covered hummocks, over the unseen marsh and jungle beyond, and down into the distant sea. The two slender, curlyheaded figures dipped and curved, weaving a net of air to pull the Sun down. Where other wide eyes drooped, theirs sparkled, and their pointed ears pricked out to hear the flute's least sigh.

When the dance was done, little old Singer took up Lobb's harp, raised a wrinkled hand, and even the dickerees chattering in the rockwood tree fell still.

First Singer sang, as she did each Feast Day, the oldest Songs: those from the Times Before. The clear, silvery thread of her voice spun its web about the gathered Tiddi, and it seemed as if the grass itself had stopped its rustling to hear the Lay of the Makers.

> *Seven the Makers, the Shapers of will—*
> *Nima the songsmith, Kyth, Giva and Rill,*
> *Rina the healer, and Ellem and Gwill—*
> *Seven the Makers, the Givers of skill.*

Temma rocked her baby to the Song's chant. Issa the Queen rested happily in the circle of Nee's arms, and Cat, sitting hunched on the outer edge of the Circle, dreamed of strange folk and strange places, her eyes wandering along the sky's edge. Across the Circle young Fith sat with his tiny pet owl Tootoo on his shoulder and his legs outstretched. Leaning back with his weight upon his palms, he felt the world tremble under his hands and took it for the tingle of his own excitement over the Tales to come. Now, he listened avidly.

Kyth on his lone under Timmerill Hill,
Stonefinder, gem shaper, tam—er . . .

The word broke in the middle on a jangle of harp notes. Singer rose, her mouth a little soundless O, and pointed with a bony finger.

Westward, beyond the distant marsh and jungled shore, the sky flashed queerly green, then faded as a swift, cold mist swept the sunset colors from the sky.

"Nar! Look to the horses!" shouted Issa the Queen as one mare cried out in a thin, whickering scream and the hooves of the others beat against the fence poles.

"The sea," Cat whispered, unbelieving. "I hear the sea!"

"The sea?" Temma hugged the baby, Little Mouse, to her breast. "But the Sunset Sea is thirty leagues away," she wailed into the rising wind.

The mist was swept away as swiftly as it came, and the sky to the west was darkened with a rush of cloud. The Tiddi heard the far-off shriek of the wind that ran before it, riding on the sea-thunder. Starwise clapped her hands to her mouth to hold in her fear and frantically searched the sky for a sign, an omen, but all the first stars of evening were swallowed up in cloud, and the moon was dim and silent. The air was filled with the angry music of wind and water.

"Oh, stars!" Issa the Queen moaned and snatched at Nee's hand. She looked around wildly for Fith, their son. "What must I do? I am only a hunter, and my spears cannot pin down the windy sea." Looking up in despair, she saw the rockwood tree.

"The tree! The tree has branches for ten times our twenty Tiddi to shelter on!"

But the rockwood was too straight boled, too high branched for even the more agile among them to climb to safety, and Issa knew it even as she spoke.

Arl, remembering tardily that he was Runner-to-the-Sky's-Edge, the chooser of ways, stirred from his daze. Pushing to the center of the Circle, he shouted, "The Wood! Run for Plum Wood. It is higher than the grass, and our beds and stores are there."

"Yes, to the Wood," Issa shrilled. "Horn, see to Skinner. Fith, *run!*"

"But—Tootoo! Where is Tootoo?"

All was confusion. Singer's grandson Horsey snatched her up in his arms and sped through the grass. Starwise hung back, looking wildly for her little bag of star-casting stones, and in that moment the wind swept over them and swallowed up their cries.

Arl, running before the gale, clutched at the stone that hung on a cord around his neck and, feeling it grow warm to his touch, took heart. His feet flew faster. Even so, the darkness overtook him and swallowed up Plum Wood, no more than a furlong ahead. He slowed, then stopped, turning to lean into the wind. The long hummock of higher ground on which the Wood stood was only yards away, for he could hear at his back the tearing shriek of the wind among the brushyplums, and the creak of heavier boughs among the redleaf trees on higher ground. His sense of direction was as sharp as a homing bird's. But what of the others, strung out through the wind-streaming grass? *And what of the World? It was sung that the Third Time was to end in drowning. Was it come, then? Was the Fourth Time to dawn without the Tiddi?* He would never see Renga again, or Lek. And never unriddle the how and why of his coming as a child to the place where Issa's folk had found him . . .

Struggling to stand against the wind, he unfolded the hand that clutched Lek's gift and saw the stone burn more brightly than ever it had, even in his dreams. As he looked, the stone's red fire shimmered even more brightly, and dark shapes moved at its center. Wrenching the cord over his head, he wrapped it around his wrist and held it high, a red firefly dancing against the wind. It was a tiny beacon, but it might serve. He plunged up through the brushyplum fringe of the Wood and found the old rockwood that leaned out to shadow the plain's edge. Thick-branched and crooked, it clutched him safe against the wind as he climbed. Once above the tops of the brushy-plums, he wrapped one arm around a stout branch and with his free hand held the blazing stone aloft.

They straggled up the little slope in twos and threes, Potter and Nar bearing up Old Nar their father between them, Horsey bringing Singer, and running down again to call into the wind for Qara and young Minnow. Horn came carrying old Skinner pick-a-back. Nee and Issa hand in hand. Harr and Temma and Little Mouse. Then, strung all together with the ropes from the horse pen, the three little horses and Fith and Holly, Starwise and Plim, Qara and Minnow.

"Adi! Where is Adi?" Arl the Runner shouted to Fith, who climbed to join him. The wind whipped the words away, but Fith understood.

"Minnow says she was holding to the rope, but she fell." Fith leaned close to shout in his friend's ear. "Cat must have gone back after her. The rope was Cat's idea. She rode at its tail, and must have seen old Adi slip."

To Issa, counting heads below, Minnow's mother, Plim, told the same tale, adding with a wail that they were surely lost. The wind was too strong. Adi could never stand against it. If only Cat had another bit of rope—

Issa nodded into the darkness, and with a hand on Plim's shoulder signed that she had heard. Then, as she gathered her breath for a great shout, the wind suddenly shrieked away east, leaving only a hissing sound, over which her cry was clearly heard: "Olders on the store platform, youngers in the trees. *Now!*"

She singled out Nee and Nar and Horn to see that all obeyed—and swiftly—and then turned to peer anxiously out into the seething darkness. Fith and Arl, above her head, heard the crashing through the brushyplums before she did. They scrambled down just as Cat came racing up the bank with old Adi the cook upon her back, bearing her as easily as if she were a child. At Issa's gruff command—and Fith's anxious tug upon her sleeve—Cat followed quickly after him and Arl toward the grove at the Wood's heart. There a store-platform was lashed high among the trees to keep the Tiddi supply of food baskets and bundles of winter clothing safe from the damp, and from hungry bears or piggars. They handed Adi up to reaching hands and hurried on to a tall lolu tree close by. Its silky bark was slippery when bruised but its branches grew down to the ground spiral-fashion, so that even in the storm's darkness they could climb quickly to a safe perch.

A lashing rain came in the wake of the wind, but it was soon past, and the storm's din with it. Behind came a strange, silken roar. At the sound of it, many of the little folk perched in the branches of Plum Wood shut their eyes in terror, but Fith strained to see. As a few bright stars broke free of the clouds, he pointed and cried out. "The sea!"

For it was the sea: a silver-crested wall of water glimpsed only for a moment before clouds once more swallowed up the starlight. Higher than an Iceling was tall, thrice as tall as any Tiddi, swifter than an elope, it was upon and past them, churning into foam where it met the banks of the wooded hummock, then spreading through the trees and away across the plain.

6. OVER THE TREETOPS

BY DAWN THE STORM had passed beyond Aye across the plains of southern Yold and crossed the Outer Sea, where by nightfall it would lash the shores of distant Umeár at Aybul.

At first light the Tiddi youngers in the trees climbed down to perch near the sapling-woven platform that held their stores and elders.

"Have *you* seen Tootoo?" Fith called softly to his mother.

Issa shook her head. "But do not worry. The wind cannot have swept her so far that she cannot fly home again."

"How is Singer-of-Tales? And Skinner and Adi? And Old Nar?" chimed the others.

"Old Nar is already grumbling for his mornmeal," Issa said. But her smile was strained. "Skinner has the trembles, and Adi cannot wake him. I think she has taken no hurt from her fall, but Skinner is frail, and I fear she will lose him. Ah, here is Young Nar," she said as Nar's head poked up over the platform's edge. "What of the horses?"

Nar shinned up the cornerpost tree and stood to shake the water from him like a beast. His legs were muddy to the knees. "All of the ropes held but one," he announced. "We lost a mare, the littlest one, swept off her feet and drowned. Had the water come two hands higher, we would have lost them all."

"Poor little mare," Issa mourned, but then she straightened her back, at once more stern and queenly, and looked around her briskly. "Tonight we will take counsel whether to stay or go on to Saan, even though it is seven weeks and three days short of the Wandereve. For now—" She clapped her hands upon her knees. "Since we cannot dance the Sun up knee-deep in mud and cannot leave Plum Wood until the water returns to the sea, we must see to making ourselves comfortable. There will be more room here on the platform if we hang our sacks and baskets in the trees. We—" She broke off at seeing Starwise raise a nervous, fluttering hand.

"Yes, sister?"

"Perhaps," said Starwise, "we cannot dance in the mud here, where there is no good footing. But still, we can sing."

The older Tiddi murmured their agreement—even Skinner, awake now and lying weak upon his pallet.

"Perhaps," Adi put in timidly, "after we have sung the Sun dance, Singer might chant a praise to Tinnel the Wolf Star. The others left us to the storm, but not Tion's star! I saw him a-twinkle through the Plum Wood trees, else I'd be dreaming under water now."

"So would we all," Horsey said.

"But it was Arl's stone, not Tinnel!" piped up Qara's clear voice.

Issa's thick brows lifted in astonishment, and she turned to stare at Arl and the small, pierced shard of stone he wore upon a thong around his neck.

Her sister Starwise padded to the edge of the platform to peer up at Arl on his perch. "The Man gave you it?" Arl nodded.

Starwise's excitement raised a snort from Old Nar. "You're thinking it a sliver of Skystone? The Tinnelstone? That it broke, and this is a bit of it? Well, it wasn't broken. There's no such a thing in the Tales."

Old Skinner raised a feeble hand from his pallet. "It's the telling makes a tale. Where there's secrets, there's no songs. It did shine lovely bright . . ."

Young Nar frowned. "This Lek—this Man—may be he thieved it. Arl says his own folk think he thieved Nirim the Worldstone."

Nee exchanged a worried glance with Issa his wife. "That is so."

"No!" Arl clutched the stone on its cord. It was now no more than a shard of mottled red and brown, and suddenly he wanted desperately for it not to be Tinnel. "He never took Nirim. And this came from his mother's folk. He told me so."

Issa saw the indignation that had sprung into his vivid young face reflected in Cat's eyes, and her own son Fith's. She held up a hand to still the talk. "Come, we are frogs on a lily pad quarreling over what an elope thinks! Arl has taken the Man for a truthteller. So must we for now. For the stone's light, we give thanks. But now we must make plans for tomorrowday."

By the morrow the water had slipped away some distance toward the Sunset Sea, but it left a sea of mud behind. The sun returned to a cloudless sky to shine so brightly that the air shimmered. By the third day the mud grew a crust, and on the fourth it began to crack. On that day Nee and the hunters went scouting east and north. In four days they returned to tell that at its height the storm had drawn the sea across the whole of the south of Yold, even the wide midland that had not seen the sea since the One Land was lifted up in the First Time. There sandy soil overlay deep limestone, and everywhere the shallow hollows of that country were filled with shining water.

Arl, gone scouting to the west, found the Tiddi skin-and-willow fishing boats hanging in the branches of the rockwood tree beside the mud-filled song circle. They had been left tied together on the River Ayakka's bank on the eve of the feast day. When he reached the river itself, he found a broad estuary where there had been only a meandering stream. The northward track that had followed the coast of the Sunset Sea was drowned.

Scouting north along the new coast, Arl puzzled, as he had for days, over his bit of red stone and Adi's taking it for the Wolf Star. Tinnel, Tion's star. So many tales, unravelled, led back to Tion, the elvish King of ancient Aam . . .

What if his stone *were* a fragment of the Tinnelstone, the Skystone that stood for red Tinnel, the Wolf Star? The Tinnelstone was believed to have gone safely to the Aldarin at the fall of Tion's Aam—to Basadil, the Silvrin King in Avel Timrel, most likely, and from there to Thamor, beyond the North. But if it had not? From Teran the Mortal, Tion's son who was King in Aam after him, it would have gone to Arrn, Teran's son. Arrn, "Tion the Second." Arrn of the sorceress wife. Arrn the Greedy of Power, corrupting Men and beasts alike and defying the Silvrin in his hatred and envy of their skills and powers and their blood that ran so thinly in his own veins. The crown and the Tinnelstone were his. When he chose death atop his blazing tower in the hour that Aam fell, would he have left the Stone and its powers for Basadil to bear away to his elvish kin on the isle of Thamor beyond the Outer Sea? Hardly.

Or—would he smash it, defiant to the end? That sounded more like King Arrn. And there might be half a hundred ways Lek's bit could have made its way to Umeár.

Arl looked down at the dull-reddish splinter of opal with a new awe. If it were a bit of the Tinnelstone, its smooth-worn edges had come from the touch of perhaps a thousand hands down the long age since Aam's fall . . .

Arl's long stride quickened.

"The sea laps against Frog Hummock and Ghostflower Wood, and all the creeks are bays," Arl told Issa on his return.

"We can go north by an inland way," the hunters said. "The deer who gained High Wood before the sea came have left there. Their footprints mark a straight track northeast, so there is good land Tha-wards."

"It is too long a journey to go to Saan by way of Tha," Plim objected. "Think of the olders."

Old Nar was offended. "Olders, indeed! But such a road will not do. We must keep to the Wandering Way, or as near it as we can." He looked to Singer-of-Tales and Adi who nodded their agreement.

"How can we, when the Way is drowned?" Issa snapped impatiently. "We must make for Saan the best way we can, and soon. We are hunters in a beastless land, and fishers without nets."

"Aye," Old Nar grumbled. "We would have been better off without the counsel of the Wolves of Aam—and these three." He scowled at Arl and Fith and Cat. "Bidding us leave Tha in Mirimoon and come here a hundred days too soon!"

Issa chided him for his ill humor. "And if we had left on the proper Wanderday? Count it out on your fingers. A week ago, on Loorimoon Eve when the sea came, where would we have been? Most likely sleeping in the Great Grass with not a tree for miles."

Everyone kept silence while Issa thought—even Star-wise, who quietly cast her star pebbles on a folded blanket but could read no sense in the patterns they made. For once she had no advice to give and twisted her fingers nervously while her sister Issa frowned and tapped her fingertips together. At last, Issa nodded. Her frown lightened, shading suddenly into laughter. She clapped her hands upon her knees.

"Ha! Of *course*. Arl is eager for news of the conjuror and his Wolf-friend, so we shall go by the swiftest way. Fith is always longing for adventure, and so we shall go a new way. And since Old Nar mistrusts all things new, we shall go by the old Way."

Old Nar blinked. The others stared and exchanged puzzled glances. Fith jiggled excitedly on his perch, and Arl's eyes held a merry glint.

Starwise was most surprised of all. "The starstones spelled out just such a riddle: 'We must follow the Wandering Way through the treetops to Saan.' But how can that be so?"

At hearing the starstones' counsel, Issa looked doubly pleased with herself. "It is simple enough. Arl tells us that the manglo forest that marched north along the seacoast marches still, a treetop thicket far out beyond the sea's new shore. Our Wanderway to Saan led under that forest's eaves. And now we shall skim above them. Why else would the stars hang our fishing scallops safely up in the rockwood tree?"

Fith had not laughed since the disappearance of the little owl Tootoo, but now he joined the two younger children in a shrill Tiddi warble of delight. Even solemn Cat's face twitched into a smile.

Old Singer clapped her hands. "Issa of the Treetops! Such a journey will make a song for your grandchildren's grandchildren to sing!"

"A brave enough idea," Old Nar said grudgingly. Nee and Plim and several of the others hid their smiles at such sour praise, but young Harr the hunter laughed outright.

Adi fretted about the stores. "What of all my baskets of nuts and seeds? My sacks and sacks of dried plums, and meat, and shrimps?"

"We will take them," Issa said briskly. "We will take the horses, too. We will take everything!"

For the horse-raft two tall lolu trees were felled, then cut in threes and carried, six hunters to a log, to the sea's muddy new shore. With choke-vines for rope, and poles and rails of rockwood, they built a raft like Lobb's raft in the Legends, with a pointed prow and simple rudder, and set a stout horse pen in the middle. The pen they heaped roundabout with bulging sacks and brim-full baskets. Horn split rockwood for paddles, and Holly and Plim shaped them and bound the handles with leather cord.

On the tenth day after the great storm, old Skinner died in a dream of horses' manes and tails a-flicker in the golden grass of an autumn mountain meadow, a dream that came when his fever broke. The Tiddi wrapped him in his finest skins and wove a stout canopy of twigs and branches to shelter him from birds and beasts and left him sleeping high in the whispering branches of Plum Wood.

The eleventh day saw five fishing scallops and a raft with seven rowers set out across the shallow Sunset Sea.

That first morning was all clear sky, pale sun and glassy water. It was Qara, trailing her hand in the water, who first spied in the raft's shadow the familiar plain below, where long grasses stirred at their passing. As the water deepened, all of Aye slid under them and away: paths and brushy hummocks, reed and flower, fishing nets strung out never to dry, and the streamless River Ayakka.

At sunset the little flotilla came among the tops of the

manglo forest. Tying their vessels fast, the Tiddi made a space amidst the baggage on the raft so that Holly might dance the Sun down for them. And then they hung their hammocks in the treetops and slept.

In the days that followed there were times when the sea forest spread across their path, a maze of little bays and confusing currents, but always, the Wandering Way under the jewel-clear water led them aright. Many a tree that had shaded them in other years on other Wanders to Saan gave them safe harbor now, and more than once they slung their hammocks in a treetop where they had hung before. The sunken, tangled forest was a barrier, too, against the sea's swell, checking its surge so that the heavy raft did not pitch or roll as Old Nar had prophesied, but each day made good headway. Where the Tiddi rowers went the sea seemed a lagoon, and the two hundred leagues to Saan a pleasant outing.

The days on the water were filled with songs and fishing, sore shoulders for the paddlers, and basket fishing for shrimps so excellent that only the little horses, whose daily ration of grain grew smaller and smaller as the baskets emptied, were discontented. For the Tiddi the journey was a floating feast, and at its end Singer sat enthroned amid the sacks of sun-dried game and fish, all still untouched.

Saan too was drowned, from the Great Reef and Fishfull Bay past the song circle on its headland, and inland beyond the broad valley of the Fishfull River and Tall Tree Swamp. On the eighteenth day of Loorimoon, the seventh day after their setting out, the sea raft and its five little outriders of hide and willow threaded among the drowned and dying lirri trees and came aground beneath an old malin, whose branches had for half an age sheltered Tiddi on the Wandering Way from Saan to Min.

"We shall call it New Saan," said Issa, first ashore.

"*Cr-rr-ruk!* And about time you got here!" croaked a harsh, familiar voice from among the malin leaves overhead.

"Hlik!"

"And *Tootoo!*" cried Fith, spying the tiny owl perched aside the great raven on the malin's branch.

"*Pr-rk*, yes. I found her five leagues upriver, calling for you. But there will be time enough later for greetings," Hlik said briskly. "I bring urgent news from Findral and the conjuror. I left them in Aabla two days ago."

7. TO THE FENNETHELEN

Findral enjoyed the hunting and lazy days in Aabla, but Lek chafed to be off again, to see the snows melt, to glean some sense from the ramblings of Hlik's vanishing magician.

"Uval Garath—" Lek said. "The Opal Mountain. Is it far from Avel Timrel?"

The old Man seemed not to hear. He touched his bandaged head and then reached out to pluck at Lek's sleeve. "Did I tell you? Once an Aldarin city stood here. A Silvrin city, to be precise. The Silvrin are darker of hair and paler of skin than the Aldarin . . . I have forgot what I was saying. Ah, yes! This bit of pretty pavement I have uncovered here—it is not a floor, as I see you suppose, but a roof. In those days summers here were long and fierce, but a buried house is cool on the hottest day. And gardens! All Aabla was a garden then . . . Did I tell you?" His fingers trembled at the knot of the grimy bandage that bound his head as if he wondered why he wore it.

The Wizard—if Wizard he was—was far from young despite his raven hair. It was not so much the white threads in his beard or the wrinkled cheeks and hands that spoke of age, but the clear gaze of his deep eyes, which seemed to see through and beyond what they rested on. Tall, shabbily dressed in a mended gown and moth-eaten cloak, he was not at all the figure of mystery or mastery Lek had looked to find. Yet now and again his vague, transparent gaze sharpened to a hawk's bright glare, and his tongue grew sharp to match it. At those times Lek thought of him as Sharp-Eyes, but more often it was as Muddlewit, a name he had to bite back more than once.

"Uval. Garath," Lek insisted, for what seemed the four-and-twentieth time, masking his impatience.

"Uval Garath?" It was Sharp-Eyes who turned to skewer the Man at his side with a hard, searching glance. "The Opal Mountain is forbidden to Men. If I knew of it, would I betray it to you for the asking?" With a return of uncertainty, he looked around him anxiously. "This *is* Aabla? Not some counterfeit?"

"I am a conjuror, not a sorcerer to cast false scenes upon the mind."

"Aha! A conjuror!" The Old Man spoke fiercely, but then as if he had lost hold of the thought that struck him, his eyes wandered to the river's edge and he said vaguely, "I met a conjuror not long ago. A lad who studied with Azra the Wise." Frowning, he sat down shakily on a nearby heap of rubble. "His name was Lark . . . Leek? Or was it Kell?"

Fearing the snappish retort that Lek's scowl threatened, Findral spoke up quickly. "His name is Lek, now, Master . . . Wizard. It was Kell when he was a boy, before the Nirimstone was stolen. He told you."

The old Man scarcely heard. It was the name that he fastened on. "Wizard? Yes. Indeed, yes, I seem to have some skill at wizardry. But no name. Can I be Gactan? No, he is dead, I think . . . Maddar? Barelly? No . . . *Orrin?* Now, *that* sounds more like the name I have been trying to lay my tongue to. Orrin . . . Yet . . . I fear one of the outlaws who tried to carry me off to Gzel gave me a

crack on my pate that has left me a trifle muddled . . .
with my own staff, the villain! My head feels leaky as a
sieve." His bushy brows drew together in a scowl of concentration. "Orrin, historian and geomancer, once of
Umeár. Am I he? I think not. No. The name seems an ill
fit. I cannot think *who* I am. But you, my friend—there is
no mistaking a Wolf of Aam."

"I am Findral, of the line of Renga, Rovanng and Ras-
sil," Findral explained, not for the first time.

"Are you alone or outcast, Findral son of Renga, that
you have taken to traveling with a Man? I see your mark
upon his face. A riddling pair!"

Lek's fingers touched the fading scar that raked across
his brow, and he smiled. "It is Findral's mark, and if I did
not have it, I would be buried deep at the foot of the
Fennethelen. The Shadow darkened my eyes as I stood in
the path of an avalanche, and Findral struck me from
it."

"Shadow?" The Wizard's gray gaze took on a queer intentness, and his hearers felt something of the power that
his confusion had let slip. "The Fennethelen? How came
you there? If that is the only scar you brought from under
the Shadow, then fortune walked with you."

When he had heard the tale of that long journey once
again, the Wizard sat with his hands upon his knees and
peered at Lek as if from a great distance. "Young Man, I
do not wholly trust the purpose that drew you there, for
while you may be honest, your heart is shadowed. Not
from your faring into the Shadowlands, I judge, but by
the thing you say you lost in Umeár. As for the Shadow, I
think you do not know the danger you escaped."

He stood and paced a little up and down—quite solid,
though Findral still hoped to see another such accidental
vanishing as Hlik told of. At length the Wizard murmured, "My, oh!" cocking his head like a curious bird to

peer at Lek. Lek was of two minds whether that intent and measuring look was the great owl's merciless and calculating stare at some small hawk that trespassed on his domain, or a raven's bright, assessing gaze.

Suddenly the old Man snapped his fingers. "Ollo! *Ollo.* Hah, yes! I am called Ollo." He sounded much relieved, and quite positive. "It *is* most unsettling to have lost one's name. I must not forget 'Ollo' again. And now, young Kell, show me your hands."

"My—?"

"Your hands. Is it so alarming a request?"

Findral saw Lek flush darkly and draw himself up haughtily, and feared a sharp retort that might shatter the old Man's self-command and set his mind to wandering again. But Lek, though his mouth tightened, held out his hands, palms up.

The Wizard's command, thought Findral, was no odder than the fact that when Lek went ungloved, one hand should always be clenched or hidden in a pocket. The palm —Findral had glimpsed it on the day the Tiddi, Wolves and Icelings rescued Lek from Gzel—was badly scarred as if by fire, but it was the right hand. Since Lek was left handed, it had seemed no great matter. Now with left and right held side by side, he saw that the right was also much the smaller. Even so, and despite its cruel scars, it was strong and shapely.

An echo stirred in Findral's mind—some word or phrase from an old Wolf Song too faintly heard for memory to seize upon. From the proud, defiant face Lek showed the Wizard it seemed that he, at least, judged his own hand shameful. A sad and foolish prejudice but, to be fair, not only a human folly. Beasts as well as Men made outcasts of their misshapen fellows.

"Oh, my, oh," the Wizard murmured to himself.

Lek shrugged as if it were no matter. "Many of my

forefolk were left-handy. It was said that my grandfather and his grandfather before him had just such a hand as this."

The Wizard pulled absently at his beard. Abruptly, he said, "There are no more wizards in Umeár. Azra was the last before the Outlawing. How did you come to be apprenticed to him?"

Lek almost smiled. "You hear more, Master Ollo, than you seem to listen to. For answer, I can only say he chose me."

"Did he not ask to see your hands?"

"He did." Lek regarded Ollo with a new interest. "Before he chose me."

"Strange. Most strange."

"No doubt," Lek said grimly; and then boyishly, hurt winning over pride, he burst out, "Why do you mistrust me? I had no hand—right or left—in Nirim the Worldstone's vanishing. I swear it."

Ollo made a gesture as if to brush aside such a thought. When he did speak, his voice was weary. "It is a long tale, and much of it uncertain. There may be no wizards left in Umeár, but here in Astarlind there seems to be one greater than any wizard. The Men who carried me off into the Empty Lands called him their Lord, and in whispers named him Naghar. He had sent them out in search of Mirelidar, the Moonstone that gave Avel Timrel its name —*Te Aveli te Mirel Issur Garath*, The City of the Moon Under the Mountain." He sighed. "I fear the Shadow that has been growing there this Age past means that the pleasant halls where Basadil's folk dwelt and danced now shelter some dark evil. And now I have heard your tale, I wonder if by some great deceit its Lord did not steal Nirim the Worldstone too."

"But it was stolen from my hands, with no one near save the King! It was done by sorcery, but I had no part in it."

"That I believe," Ollo said. "Yet . . . I have seen such hands more that once before, and know a better reason to mistrust them than Umeáran superstition." The Wizard's face was grave. " 'Arrn's Hand'," the Aldar call it."

Ollo did not explain. He seemed not to notice the conjuror's dismay at the name of King Tion's grandson, Arrn, whose pride caused Aam's destruction. It appeared that only a great effort of will had held his mind to Lek's tale. He said wearily, "Uval Garath and Avel Timrel lie at the heart of the Fennethelen. The one lies within the other: the City within the Mountain." As he sank back into his bed of boughs, his gaze wandered and grew vacant. To Lek's anxious questioning he mumbled only, "I must be gone. I am waited for in Avella." Once he made as if to rise and, looking about him in confusion, cried out weakly, "Why have I pottered here among these broken stones when there is work to do?"

Lifting Ollo from his chair, Lek carried him to the bed of dried ferns and green pine boughs under the lean-to. "He is as light as if his bones were hollow, like a bird's." Opening the leather box at his belt, Lek took out a small flask. "There's little more than a swallow left. And though I have ointment for a cut scalp, it will not heal a cracked head."

Findral watched the drowsing Wizard rouse to drink from the flask Lek held to his lips. "What shall we do? He needs care and close watching. I wish it were Trillimoon Eve. Rovanng and Renga and all the Wolves of Aam would be here."

Lek looked up from bandaging Ollo's head afresh. "Trillimoon! That's not four days hence. Yet even four days . . . If spring already touches Aabla, snow-melt must come before many weeks to the mountains, even mountains under the Shadow. If I tarry for this addlepated Wizard,

60

Avel Timrel may well be lost again. The way we came will not be the same. Deep-drifted valleys and great snow-fields without their snow can match a Wizard's trans-formations. Even mountain peaks change their faces when spring takes away their masks of ice and snow. I cannot wait here! If our Tiddi friends are not here by now, they must mean to join us at Baggal's Spring."

"Go, then. I will wait here for my folk," Findral said. "Then, if Rovanng and Renga do not forbid it, I will follow. Look for me before the middle day of the new month."

Lek made haste across the great "island" of Aabla, carrying Ollo's feather-light boat upon his back. Eastward, across the gentle hillslopes, he was pleased to see snow among the tussocks of the old year's grass, and more thickly in the hills' folds and in the shadows of the golden malin groves. Along the island's eastern shore the Neea, unlike its wide, calm western channel, ran deep and swift. The Wizard's little boat skimmed across as lightly as if the tumbling river were a duckpond in Alladar and Lek as light as the boy he once was. Stepping ashore, with a command he sent it sailing back to the shelter of the willow tangles along the Aabla bank.

At Riversmeet two days later, Lek followed the River Onga as it flowed north through the rolling snow plains of ancient Aabla, and then turned east along the stream Findral had guessed to be the Kithka. This lesser river wound through the Rumples into the bleak, hunched hills north of the Shadowlands. Some four leagues before the Kithka bent through the foothills into the Shadowlands, it was joined by the swift creek that flowed down from Baggal's Spring. There a long-abandoned trail threaded south to meet the path along the westernmost ridge of the Blue Mountains. By traveling far into the night and rising before the moon set, Lek reached Baggal's Spring on the sixth day of Trillimoon.

Hlik and Cat and Arl and Fith arrived there two days later.

While Arl and Lek talked, Fith shivered in the chill crosswinds that blew down from the Owl Mountains far to the North, and from those other mountains, muffled up in shadow, that barred the Fennethelen from the daylight world. If he felt dismay at such a darkness and so deep a distance, he did not dare admit it. He felt very young and very small. But at least he and Tootoo were warm. The three Tiddi had carried their snow-bear coats of Iceling make from Eem to Tha and on to Aye atop already heavy burden sacks, in defiance of the others' smiles. Now they were glad of it.

"Can't we go? He stamped his feet and felt the little owl flutter in alarm inside his coat, then nestle down again against his breast. Tonight would be soon enough to bring her out. After dark. Lek would not be pleased at taking a useless passenger on a great venture, but if he did not see her for a day or two, they would have gone too far to send so small a creature back across the wilderness.

"Yes, come." Lek shouldered his pack and looked up at Hlik on his fringe-tree perch. "Are you coming with us, Old One?"

"Not yet," Hlik croaked. "I have business to the West and mean to stop in Aabla on the way. If I had known my vanishing Man were Ollo, whom I have not seen hereabouts since he was young and beardless, I would have paused in my errand to the Wolves in Ottamoon. But I will join you when I can. Look for me when you see me."

Lek gave him a sharp glance. "Ah. I thought you did not know where Uval Garath lay."

"*Pru-u-uk*! I did not say so. I said I had not fared be-

neath the Shadow, and that for all I know the lands there
were all reshaped at the ending of the Times Before. For
all *I* know. But I confess that I have heard from others
otherwise."

"You meant to keep me from my search? Why?"

The old raven fixed the conjuror with a stare as fathom-
less as it was black. "I feared you meddled in great dangers, all to polish a tarnished name. Your death is your
own to choose, but the Ravens of Domgrath and Findral's
folk are ancient friends, and I did not like to see a good
beast lost for no good cause."

"Have you changed your mind, then?"

Hlik flapped his great wings and, lifting from his
branch, called back, "Yes—because there is more to your
errand than you know. And more to you than meets the
eye. Ask Arl." He rose into the wind and swept away.

Lek lifted a hand to shade his eyes as he watched the
great raven dwindle to a fleck upon the sky's edge. When
he turned to his Tiddi companions, there was no reading
his face.

" 'Ask Arl,' he said. Ask you what?"

"About your bit of stone, I think. The red stone you
gave to me in Aam."

"What of it?" Lek said impatiently. "It is nothing. An
old wives' amulet for sprains and fever. A trinket."

From Lek's scowl Arl thought perhaps the mention of
any stone put him in mind of Nirim's loss. Or had Hlik's
parting speech unsettled him? Arl would have held his
tongue; but Fith was not so shy.

"Well, then, your trinket saved the Tiddi!"

Lek's impatient frown shaded into unwilling interest as
the tale of Aye's flood and the flaming stone poured out.

"I have seen it shine," he admitted. "When my mother
handled it. But only faintly, and that was long ago. I
thought it had 'died,' as opals will."

Fith's eyes shone. "We think it must be a bit of the Tinnelstone."

To his surprise, Lek flushed angrily. "So now my folk are to have stolen another of the Twelve Stones? As I am supposed to have stolen Nirim? Tell me: how could fisher-folk and farmers in Umeár come by a stone that lived in Tion's treasure house in Aam and then went to Thamor, beyond the North? If you must go inventing tales, leave me out of them!"

Fith, surprised but not abashed, would have protested, but Cat warned him to silence with a shake of her head. Had it not been too cold to take off her gloves, she would have signed, "Let him riddle it out for himself." Instead, as the Man led off up the trail with long, angry strides, she fell into an easy trot behind, and Arl and Fith came after.

They hunted as they went until, as they moved under the Shadow, their packs and sacks would hold no more. They moved on each morning with a little lighter step, for it was Lek's plan to bury a cache of meat near each night's shelter-place so that they need not go hungry on their return. Nor would they be burdened with heavy stores as they climbed toward the long-lost city under the hidden mountains.

Snow still lay in deep, hard-crusted drifts under the Shadow. The surefooted Tiddi, used to day-long runs—if in kinder weather—kept to the pace Lek set. And if it was not a cheerful journey under that heart-heavy sky, the Tiddi fared better than their companion. Lek felt the weight of the graylands on his heart even more heavily than on his first journey there. At darkfall he watched the Tiddi at their Sunset dance with shadowed eyes. After-ward he said little, but listened to their gossiping tales of friends and elders, and to their songs, as if these homely things were a comfort to him too.

On the thirteenth day out from Baggal's Spring, the companions left the steep valleys and sharp ridges behind and made their way down the broken Wolf Way to the long curve of glacier that ringed the Fennethelen's peaks. There they saw the ruin left by the fire mountain and the great earthshake that had followed. The range of peaks still stood, but in places along its curving length, the ash-gray glacier wore great fans of rubble, rock split and tumbled from far above. Great snow heaps stained it too, white splashes of ancient snow shaken out of old, deep beds in massive avalanches.

Arl was dismayed. "But—how can we find one hole in one snowbank in all this?"

Lek pointed. "It lies directly below the double peak, in line with the narrow cleft just—there! Findral and I fled as soon as it was safe to leave our cover, but we saw the avalanches had not come near it."

Nor had any since, but in the rain of warm ash, the snow of the great drift itself had slumped downward so that its shape was changed. For two hours the four companions dug with Lek's snowshoes before they found a trace of the snow creature's tunnel.

When they did, Cat sat back upon her heels. "Oh Stars," she whispered.

8. DORIL'S HOLE

THE LITTLE, HEART-SHAPED FACE beneath Cat's hand was ashy pale and peaceful. The earthshake had tumbled his tunnel's cold weight down upon him, and he had curled himself up and slipped into his final dreamless sleep.

With Lek's help the Tiddi buried the small figure as he was, curled against the crushing cold. Because all around was rock, or snow that might vanish in summer, Lek carried him out onto the glacier and they laid him in a shallow crevice there and filled it up with snow and stones.

"I have brought you a long way for a riddle without an answer," Lek said when they had finished.

Arl clapped his gloved hands together and danced a little against the cold. "He *cannot* have lived in a snowbank. No more than we could. And he was smaller. And dressed only in two shirts and two pairs of leggings stitched together. There was more stitching to them than padding."

"Come. I do not like standing out here in the open," Lek said.

When they had clambered down from the ice and stood once more at the mountain's foot, he said thoughtfully, "The cache of food he had—we made two scant meals from it. It might have lasted him for a week. No more."

"It wouldn't have seen him free of the Shadowlands—if he was storing it up against a journey," Cat said.

"He could not know that. He was escaping from the mountain." Arl shivered, as if the words "escaping from the mountain" had awakened his old dreams of darkness and deep caverns, and his parents Olf and Oona hurrying him away from—what?

Another hour's digging brought the Tiddi to the rock of the mountain's flank. There they might have stopped, for Lek in scouting down glacier had come upon a fissure in the cliff face, a cleft that angled upward toward the lower end of the broken Wolf Way high above. He was impatient to attempt the climb, but Arl could not be lured away from the digging. Fair hair, ashen skin—they were so strange, and so familiar. "There has to be a passage. There has to be," he insisted, and dug on.

There was: well hidden behind a great boulder split from the mountainside, and cunningly carved—inside there were the marks of tools—to seem a narrow, slantwise crack. It angled into darkness.

Arl sat panting in the snow while one by one the others knelt to peer inside. "I knew," he said dreamily. "It had to be here. Doril's Hole. The youngles spoke of it in whispers, but no one knew where it was. This is Doril's Hole!" He shook his head as if in a daze.

Fith and Cat turned toward him in surprise and Lek, after a moment's blank stare, reached down to seize Arl by the shoulder. "Youngles? Doril's Hole? What do you know of this place? Who is Doril? Do you know, or do you play another Tiddi guess-game?" He gave Arl a sharper shake than he had meant, forgetting how much his strength overmatched a Tiddi's.

"Ow!" With a quick twist and a wriggle, Arl was free. "Doril's Hole. Doril's Hole," he muttered to himself, as if the sound of the name might waken other memories.

Fith and Cat were as eager as Lek to know what it could mean, but they knew that once broken, Arl's waking dreams were gone. They came will-you, nil-you, and slipped away in the same fashion.

"No matter," Fith said. "It will come. *I* want to have a look inside."

Cat, crouched by the cleft, pulled off a glove to hold her hand out to its darkness. "Strange. The air seems almost warm."

"Yes. Because it's winter," Arl said slowly. "There was a rhyme my mother sang . . .

"Summer, summer, wrap up well,
It's warm outside, the Legends tell.
But cold still rules in Everdark.

Winter, winter, back go bare,
For skin will mend where shirts will tear.
A deep, warm lair is Everdark."

"Everdark!" Fith drew back a little from the cleft. "Is this the way to Everdark, then?"

"Doril's Hole, and now Everdark?" Lek said. "Another tale of might-be-could-be! But it makes no matter. Even if it were a straight road through to Avel Timrel, I am too long and broad to follow it. I am for . . ." But having got so far, he checked himself, and looked down at Arl uneasily.

"This place you were taken from as a child, this Everdark—Do you still flee from it in your dreams? And how did the rhyme go with the song you sang us on the road back from Gzel?"

"I know only a bit of it," Arl said. "I must have overheard it—many voices, singing very softly. As if it were a secret song. I remember that it frightened me." He looked far off down the ice river's sweeping curve and half sang, half whispered,

> *Goblin soldiers,*
> *Wheel and march*
> *Before the gates*
> *Of Everdark,*
> *Where trees are stone*
> *And water glass,*
> *Where no day dawns*
> *And no nights pass.*
> *In Everdark*
> *No flower fades . . .*

Lek turned to scan the ice and the shadowed ridge they had crossed that morning. " 'Goblin soldiers'? The Rokarrhuk are soldiers, right enough, though 'goblin' is a word as new to me as the creatures themselves. When Findral and I came down from the north, we saw a troop of them heading toward the Owl Mountains. They had a straggling, much-traveled look, so we supposed them homeward-bound to Nagharot. Now I am not so sure. If their Master's kingdom Nagharot and your Everdark are by misfortune the same, and lie under the Fennethelen, then more dangers than rock and snow and hunger lie between us and Avel Timrel. I meant to offer you a puzzle, and instead I give you peril. Old Hlik was right."

Cat drew herself up to her full height and gave the conjuror a look of mingled reproach and scorn. Even bundled in a bearskin coat and heavy boots she showed an easy confidence Arl and Fith had not seen in her before.

"You should have told us you saw the goblin beast-Men. Did you think we would not come? Well, we would have.

Fith and I have fought the Rokarrhuk. If we had known, we would have brought extra hunting spears. And a sackful of sleep darts instead of a few pocketsful."

Lek gave her a startled, curious look. The Tiddi were small enough that he slipped all too easily into thinking of them as children, when not even Fith, at twelve the youngest, was a child in the sense that a twelve-year-old would be on comfortable Umeár. Even so, Cat was . . . different.

"Were there Dread Ones with them?" Fith burst out. "The giant wolves?"

Lek shook his head. "I saw none. Nor did Findral, and by his telling the Wolves of Aam have sharp eyes for their ancient enemies."

Fith brightened. "Ho, that's good! I don't mind Rokarrhuk half so much as the Dread Ones. And it would be a pity to turn back now, when there may be a new folk to add to the Lists. Ashen-skins? Ashkins! They could know tales we—" He paused, struck by a dismaying thought. "What if we find more of them, and they don't speak the Old Speech? How will we learn who they are? How will we learn their Songs?"

"Or whether they mean to be friends," said Cat more practically.

"I don't know about the Old Speech, but I—I think they must speak Tiddrin," Arl said unexpectedly. The anxious, troubled frown he had worn from the moment Cat first brushed the snow from the small, frozen face of the Ashkin, as Fith had named him, deepened. "Whether they will count us friends, I do not know, but they *are* Tiddi."

"Tiddi? But his skin! His hair. And him so small!" Cat added the last in spite of herself, for her head was in a whirl. Could one be half Tiddi and half else? Was that why Lek watched her so intently?

"I don't understand why it should be so," Arl said

slowly. "I only know it from my dreams, and I know dreams can cobble truth into a lie. But when I close my eyes and remember the cavern's darkness, and Oona's tiny lamp, and myself astride my father Olf's back, I cannot see them clearly. But it has always puzzled me that I see his hair shining fair against the light. And she is a pale shadow at its edge. Not her garment—all of her. Her hair was pale as a cloud upon the night sky."

Fith was awed into silence by this new strangeness in his friend.

"A riddle within a puzzle within a mystery," murmured Lek. He stared up at the dark peaks.

Cat's eyes shone. "Perhaps the answer to one unriddles all the others. The rest of you may stay and debate until nightfall, like true Tiddi. *I* mean to see where little Ashkin came from."

It was agreed that while the Tiddi explored the narrow passage, Lek would try to gain the ancient path threading up the face of the passless Fennethelen. A road a paw's-width narrow, Findral had said, but then Findral's paw was wider than a Man's foot, and Lek was sure-footed. If the passage led the Tiddi beneath the mountain range and out the other side, they were to seek out the Wolf Way's end by tomorrow sundown. If they could not meet, all would retrace their steps and together try to find some other way.

Cat knelt and, pushing her carrying sack ahead of her into the passage, wriggled out of sight. Arl, eager and fearful, came close behind, and Fith was last.

"If we have to crawl all the way under the mountain," said Fith, "we'll wear our knees right through, not just our leggings."

The faint light that seeped in past the barrier rock at the entrance was enough for Tiddi eyes. They could see

71

the rough, chipped surface of the dark rock that pressed close above and on each side. Gradually—it was a while before they noticed it—the passage tilted gently upward. Looking back, Fith could see not even a glimmer of the light behind. Their scuffling movements had taken on an echo, as if the passage widened not far ahead. Cat stopped, and Arl heard her rummage in her sack.

"The air is almost still here," Arl whispered.

"I have a bit of candle," Cat muttered. "One brought back from Gzel . . . ah, here it is!" Fishing in a deep pocket, she brought out her sparkstones and the little pouch of dry moss for making fire. In a moment she had struck a spark into the moss and coaxed it to a bright glow. A touch, and the candle wick grew a tiny bead of flame to be cupped in her hands until it lengthened and flecked the chipped black, glassy rock with a hundred golden lights.

Cat held the candle high and gave her sack a push ahead. "Look, it's not so low up— Hai! What was that?"

"My sack bumped into Arl's boots," Fith said.

"No, it was a—squeak."

"I heard it too," Arl said. "A bat."

The air had grown steadily warmer, but at the thought of bats Cat shivered and pulled her fur hood down over her brow as she scrambled erect. Her head bumped the roof, and she hunched down a little as she moved forward. But there the roof was higher. "It's wider, too, and the walls have been smoothed."

"Stranger and stranger," Fith said.

A few yards further along they came upon a deep niche —almost a small chamber—on the right, where a number of worn tools, many of them broken, lay in heaps against the walls.

"Miners' tools! This was a mine, then," Arl said wonderingly. "It must have ended about here. And Doril cut the secret way to the outside that we have come by. It must have taken years."

Fith looked around. "If it was a mine, what did they mine?"

Arl shrugged, and Cat knelt to peer into a grimy sack that had been thrust behind a stack of tools. "Lamps! Six —seven of them! And wicks. And *oil*." She flourished a stone bottle and a small, queerly shaped stone lamp with a handle on its bottom that made it look like a small stone torch.

"We can pack the extras in our sacks," said Arl as he held a lamp for Cat to fill and trim. "Just in case."

Fith was drawn to a small heap of skins nearby. For a moment he thought it a makeshift bed, but a closer look proved them no more than scraps, stained and stiff with grime. He wrinkled up his nose and turned away to take and stow in his sack the two small lamps Cat passed to him. Arl filled a lamp for himself and lit it with Cat's stubby candle. Together they moved back into the passage.

"Why are we being so quiet?" Fith whispered.

It was the strangeness of the place, the odd deadness of sound, Arl answered in hunters' sign language. Every word, even a whispered one, was like a pebble dropped down a dark well. There was no echo, no reverberation off the glassy walls, but that very lack made them strain to hear some faint return. Even whispers slithered into silence within a yard or two. Cat, as nervous as she was brave, was thankful to be reminded that there was no need for speech.

"The lamp-glow does not carry far, and my eyes are not so night-sharp as yours," she signed to Arl. "You go first."

Further along, they passed the first of many side passages, each opening into a honeycomb of mine galleries. Fith's repeated "I wonder what they mined?" set up a hundred little echoes, as eerie as the silence they had passed through earlier. Startled, he too turned to signs.

The air grew steadily warmer as they made their way further under the mountain, and soon coats and boots followed gloves into their burden sacks. At least four hours —perhaps as many as six—had passed since they crawled into the Ashkin's passage. The three friends began to watch for a place where they might dance the unseen Sun down and Moon up, eat, and rest until the morning; but furlong after furlong they found no place wide enough. The opening to every gallery was blocked with rubble, the older workings having been filled with the tailings from newer galleries as they were cut. Two weary hours and a scanty supper later, they still pattered on.

It was Fith who spied the thin, bright thread that glimmered briefly overhead in the passing lamplight.

"Vindurn!" he cried. When Arl, some dozen yards ahead, seemed not to hear, he shouted it. "It was a vindurn mine! Come, look!"

Arl turned back and held the lamp close to see where Fith pointed. The three friends stared in awe. It was the merest thread, perhaps the last trace of a wider vein, but unmistakably pure vindurn. According to the Legends, in the First World Tiddi craftsmen had made vessels of it for the Aldar, and weapons of great beauty, but all that the Last of the Tiddi had to remind them of that vanished skill and wealth were two small knives with delicate vines laced and twined around their hafts. Arl carried one, and Cat the other.

"Vindurn! Of course. Nothing else would be worth working through black glass and solid firestone. Not even Lek's precious opals," Arl signed.

Cat's fingers flew in answer. "But they are found in firestone too. He said so."

"Not in—"

Crash!

The lamp winked out, leaving the passage in darkness, as Arl gave a yelp of pain.

"What is it?" demanded Cat and Fith together. Each reached out quickly to Arl.

"Something struck my hand. A stone, it felt like." Kneeling, he groped along the sandy floor. "Ai, the lamp is broken!"

"We have the others. And the oil." Cat rooted in her pocket again, and with the sparkstones relit her carefully saved stubbin of candle so that she could see to refill another of the small stone lamps.

Smash!

The stone bottle shattered, splashing oil, and the candle snuffed out in the sand.

"Cat?"

"Sssh! Listen . . ."

Pitpatpitpatpitpatpitpat. The sound, light as a pattering leaf-fall, grew fainter, hesitated, pit-patted on, and then stopped altogether.

"Two-legged or four?" Cat breathed.

"Four," said Fith. "Two? I'm not sure."

"Small, at least," Arl whispered. "And close still, or we could not hear it."

Wordlessly, the three Tiddi joined hands and spread across the passage, Arl and Cat on the right and left, each trailing a hand along a wall. They ran through the darkness like hunters at noon, silently, pointed ears pricked out to catch a footfall.

Instead they heard a squeak of alarm unexpectedly close at hand, and felt a spray of sand from scurrying feet. Arl made a snatch into the darkness as he ran.

"Caught it! *Ouch!*"

"What is it? What is it?" Fith cried. He reached out blindly.

Arl was panting. "I can't tell. But it's little. *Ai!* And all scratching and teeth."

It was several minutes before Cat, backtracking, could retrieve and light her candle. By its light they saw what they had caught: a fierce, little stone-throwing child. A coppery-skinned, curly-headed, woefully thin, half-naked child.

Not ashen-skinned. Unmistakably, a Tiddi child.

9. INTO THE MIST

"IT'S NOT POSSIBLE!" Fith protested as the excitement of the dark hunt faded into bewilderment. A true Tiddi who did not belong to the Last of the Tiddi? A riddle-child, like Arl and Cat had been. He had known all his life that Arl and Cat were foundlings, but had put it from his mind, for he believed the Legends and, like his elders, turned away from the riddle. Either Arl and Cat were not truly Tiddi, or Issa's little band were not truly the Last of the Tiddi. And if they were not, then Lobb the Singer had been Lobb the Liar. And if Lobb's Songs were false, what then was true? It was a wonder the elders had not left Cat to the sea and small Arl in his basket hiding-place for the beasts to eat.

"Do not be afraid." Cat knelt and spoke in the soothing voice she used with the little wild horses. "We are friends. I am Cat and this is Arl, and this Fith. What is your name? Are you alone?"

The child, struggling against Arl's grip, clenched its eyes tight shut and, letting out a cry that was half whistle, half squeak, kicked out wildly.

Cat sprang up and stood nursing her elbow. "A fierce little thing!"

"And strong for such a spindly mite," said Arl. "Aiow!"

He held the wriggling child with one hand and sucked at his wrist. "He bit me!"

"I think *she* bit you. She is frightened," Cat said.

Unexpectedly, Fith began very softly to sing. "*Star and stone . . .*

> *Star and stone,*
> *Sea and shell.*
> *Gwill has shaped*
> *A moonsong bell.*

At Gwill's name the child's struggles slowed, and by the stanza's ending she was listening intently.

> *Leaf and flower,*
> *Stem and root,*
> *Ellem tends*
> *The rainbow fruit.*
>
> *Of nut and feather,*
> *Seed and . . .*

Fith stopped abruptly and, with Arl and Cat, stared in amazement as the ragged little figure crossed her hands upon her breast and in a small, soft voice began to sing, all on one note,

> "*Onuddenvedder,*
> *Zeddenvine,*
> *Nimabrood*
> *Uhzongli gwine.*"

"Oh my stars!" said Fith.

Cat's brow furrowed. "What did she say?"

Arl answered dazedly. "She sings, '*Of nut and feather, seed and vine, Nima brews a song like wine.*' "

They rested for an hour apiece and then, each in turn again, for another hour, fearing that if they took a longer sleep, the two who watched might doze and their small captive slip away. Though she would not speak, or sing again, she had eaten ravenously every scrap they gave her, and watched intently. Her large, dark eyes scarcely blinked as she crouched down against the passage wall like a little spring wound ready to bound away the moment an eyelid drooped. If she were the child of the poor dead Ashkin, it was a marvel that after the long weeks alone she had the strength to crawl, let alone to run and kick.

At the third hour past middlenight, by Arl's guess, they took up their packs once more. Every hour saved would be another to spend on—what? The wonders of Avel Timrel, or the riddle of Everdark?

"Come, little one," Cat said. "Such a little snip of a thing! Haven't you a name? . . . No answer? Well, then, 'Snip' will have to do. I must tie this cord around your waist. I can see it in your eye that you would be off at first blink without it. There!" She made the knot fast, then tied the free ends together, to provide herself a handle. "Come."

Arl was already away, but only moments later he stopped and snuffed out his candle.

"Do you feel it? The air is colder. I think the opening may not be far off. Look."

The passage still climbed a little, but straightly, and a tiny patch of gray far off told that somewhere ahead lay an opening and the end of night. As the companions moved on, Cat wondered idly that the floor should be so sandy—that in a mine deep in fire-rock there should be sand at all. To muffle footsteps? So many long years of secret burrowing, so many hands' work, to end in a snow-bank. In the silent darkness she tightened her grip on the knotted thong, straining to hear the *pitpat, pitpat* at its end.

The vaulted mine entrance, its ceiling carved with interlacing vines like those that wreathed the old vindurn knives, was blocked from floor to ceiling by a roughhewn stone wall twelve feet thick. A narrow passage had been cut through that wall—cut through, not built into it. The outer end was cut at so sharp an angle that from any distance it must seem no more than a weathered crack.

Beyond the barrier wall, the Tiddi and their small captive found themselves on a broad, smooth ledge in the half-light of a shadowed dawn. To the left the ledge bent down along the mountain's flank, a wide road rutted with long years of use and broken in many places from long neglect. To the right the ledge curved in against the mountainside. Where it did so, a long, slanted groove had been cut downward, where carts or burden-bearers must have tipped their loads of ore, sending it down a long fall to the valley floor. That floor now was obscured by mist, but northward, to the left, a cluster of lights winked faintly. Campfires, perhaps. Or torches. The travelers could not tell. Beyond, a dark mountain-shadow reared up, greater and more sharply peaked than they had ever seen. The cloud-heavy dawn sky rode upon its shoulders and gave mist and mountain alike the look of shadows in a dream—of a world made all of lead.

Pinpricks of light—torches, most likely—curved up across the face of the mountain opposite, to a point a little lower than the entrance to the old vindurn mine where they stood. A road, or track. Fith, shivering with excitement, insisted that a tall, deep shadow between the two topmost lights hid a high, arched door. It was flanked by what looked like columns.

Arl nodded. "I see it. But the shadows are too deep to tell whether the door is open or closed or walled shut like the mine."

"It wouldn't be," Cat said, though her dark-sight was not so keen as theirs. "Not with a torchlit road leading there. Avel Timrel! Is it the door to Avel Timrel?"

"Or Everdark," Arl countered gloomily. Arl shivered, though the air, even so high above the valley, was unexpectedly warm.

"Whichever it is, our Snippet must come from there," Fith said.

"Not only Snip," Arl murmured. He could not take his eyes from the gateway into the dark mountain. The fires and torches were alarming. What could campfires mean but companies of the Naghar's soldiers?

Cat, out of the tail of her eye, watched Snip, whose ears had pricked up though her face remained blank and sullen. When Fith first spoke of the great door, she had stiffened.

"As soon as there is light enough to see that the way is clear, we must find the Wolf Way and climb to meet Lek, to warn him," Arl said.

"What are we do to with the little one?" Cat asked. "She would freeze in the snows, but how can we leave her here alone?"

"We could creep down to see whose watchfires burn below," Fith suggested. He stepped to the edge and peered downward. He counted fourteen—no, fifteen glimmers in the mist below. "We've time enough."

"*Nome! Mussen!*"

The child's great eyes were round with alarm, and she hissed the words out. "*Karragum. Lizzen!*"

Sound of morning stirrings floated up from the valley

floor, dimmed by distance and the muffling mist. Shouts came, and the clatter of iron-shod wheels and then, more and more clearly, the faint shuffle and thump of marching feet.

Cat knelt down and laid her ear to the rock. "Rokarrhuk on the mine road!" she whispered. "Can you see them? That's what 'Karragum' must mean: 'the Rokarrhuk come.'"

Fith was alarmed. "Why would they come up here? Can they have heard us?"

"From so far away? I cannot think so." Arl's voice was grim. "But even if Ashkin and his Snippet were escaping alone, others may have known of it, and tongues can be made to wag. The Naghar might have learned of this hidden passage into the mine, and of Doril's Hole. Or it may be a regular patrol. It would seem we've found not only Avel Timrel and Everdark, but Nagharot; and the sooner we lose it the better! Come!"

Fith and Cat stood rooted. The dread of just such a discovery must all along have been growing secretly in their hearts as they passed through the spirit-numbing Shadowlands, for they knew it at once for the truth. Nagharot! In Gzel they had the help of Wolves and Icelings, but here . . . three Tiddi and a Man against the whole of Nagharot?

"Dizzay! Dizzay!"

Snip tugged at her rope. "*Nommine!* Karragedyou. Go Woovay. Gumwimee. *Woovay! Gum-wi-mee!*" Pulling Cat after her, she made for the ore chute.

"*That* way?" Dismayed, Fith came to peer over the edge. "It's too steep. And smooth. What's to keep us from going the way we came? Rokarrhuk are too big to cram themselves through such a narrow opening."

"Nome! Nomine. Karrag zeeyou, zmellyou, bing virebogs, make *blam!* Make door vor Karrags. You commee."

Making a sudden lunge, Snip freed herself from Cat's grip on the thong rope and stretched out flat to reach over the edge of the deep-cut chute. One thin arm groped in the darkness below, and in the next moment Snip had wriggled around and slipped over the rim.

A fearful Cat knelt to peer after her. Arl and Fith, craning to see, were surprised to hear her soft laugh.

"It's all right," Cat whispered. "This way to the Wolf Way!"

A stout metal ring, perhaps one that had secured ore sledges, was let into the stone under the lip of the chute. From this a thin, gray rope, invisible against the rock, hung doubled. Snip was already out of sight, far down the shadowy stone trough. Cat reached down to grasp the rope, turned cautiously, and lowered herself until her feet touched the smooth side. Fith and Arl followed her example and descended swiftly, hand over hand.

It seemed a very long way going down, but looking up from the bottom—the mist there was not so thick as it had looked from above—Arl guessed it to be perhaps a furlong, no more. But a furlong doubled was a very long rope indeed.

Snip took the knotted ends from him and stretched up to tuck them into a crack nearby. It was as if the rope, knots and all, had vanished.

A watchfire flickered not far off, and hulking shadows moved around it, one among them taller, straighter. Rokarrhuk. And a Man?

Gravely, the Ashkin's child placed in Cat's hand the knotted end of the cord still tied around her waist, then made a sign to show that Cat should take Fith's hand, and Fith Arl's. When they had done so, she smiled, and led them into the mist.

II. THE MOUNTAIN

10. BEYOND THE MIST

By MIDMORNING the valley mist had retreated to the meadows bordering the river. Walking blindly in its shelter, the companions could hear the river's rush close by on the left. The fog was filled with strange echoes from far off—the hiss of water on hot coals, a snatch of speech, an owl's cry that seemed to come from far below, as if they walked not on the gravel under their feet, but high up in the air. Sometimes the river sang on their right and not on the left, even—most eerily—overhead. When Arl, in answer to a question from Fith, said, "No more than three leagues so far, if that," the answer seemed to Fith to come from ahead, not behind.

The mist made as daunting a barrier to many-peaked Avel Timrel-Nagharot as any wall of stone. The bottomlands where they walked—"meadows" was too happy a name for such gray and starveling fields—were scored with gullies, some ditch-deep, some steep ravines, that slowed even the sure-footed Tiddi.

Snip, despite her followers' impatience, kept within the border of this river mistland. "Eyes ebbaware. Favver deechmee dizzay," she insisted.

Snip's speech, the more they heard of it, was clearly recognizable as Tiddi speech, but softened and blurred. She did not whisper, but they had to strain to hear.

Muffled by the mist, her "Eyes-everywhere—Father-teach-
me-this-way," spoken in its curious monotone, was almost
lost in the murmur of the river.

Four times they splashed through shallow creeks, and a
little way beyond the fourth they heard the rush of still
another, larger stream ahead on the right. How, Arl wondered, were they to cross it if the Wolf Way lay beyond?
Yet, as they went on, it drew no nearer.

At midafternoon they found a great, flat-topped rock,
climbed it, and spread out a tardy but generous noonmeal.
Snip stared wide-eyed as Fith brought Tootoo out from
inside his coat and began to find her scraps of meat.

"We have more game than will keep," Cat said practically. "The air is too warm here. Half of mine has thawed
already. Better to make a feast than see it spoil."

Arl looked up from his portion of half-raw dabby.
"What day is this?"

"The fifteenth of Trillimoon." Fith laughed. "So this is
a midmoon feast!"

"There *is* no such thing as a midmoon feast," said Cat,
mimicking Old Nar's growl.

Snip, wolfing down the half-raw meat as if she feared
every next bite might be snatched away, stared from one
to the other of the three friends in mystification. Arl
looked around him, straining to see some feature, some
sign of the land's shape, through the leaden mist. But
beyond the rock was nothing. The sounds of the Rokarrhuk camps were left far behind; the gray world was
narrowed to a mossy rock and the rush and murmur of
unseen waters. It was a world without direction, but Arl
the Runner needed no Sun or sun-cast shadow to tell him
that time was growing short. Two hours—no more, and
perhaps less—were left before the meeting time agreed
upon with Lek.

"We had best make the rest of it a walking feast," he

said. "You, Snip! How far to the foot of the Wolf Way now?"

"Nower. Nammore." An hour. No more.

"Come, then." Arl slung his sack over his shoulder and jumped lightly to the ground. "With luck, Lek will be there before us. If we are late he will think we failed and may turn back to meet us where we parted."

"I doubt he will be there before us," Cat said. "His road is the harder and may not be passable." Slipping down to stand beside Arl, she reached up to lift down the Ashkin's child.

Fith scrambled after them and brought up the rear. He grinned. "Lek will make his way across, Wolf Way or no. I can see him hanging by his fingernails and inching toward the next toehold. All we need do is sit down by the path and wait."

"Hah!" But it would be tempting to do just that, Arl thought. The sight of Avel Timrel and the Great Gate into its halls had stirred his old dreams and fears—and a deep longing he could not put a name to. He fell into a half-dream, his mind walking among shadows in a rose-gold hall while his feet trod the mist. He followed blindly where Cat's hand drew him. When at last he woke to his surroundings, he was startled to find that they had left the misty valley floor and were climbing steadily toward a narrow vee of shadow, high between two spurs of the Fennethelen.

A steep, stony little valley lay within the shadow, and they rested there awhile. Or, Arl and Fith and Cat did. Snip, though her shoulders drooped and she stumbled now and again from tiredness, could not sit still, but ran back down a way to watch the path below. When she returned she urged them on. "Come. Dizziz Woovay you loogvor."

She watched with a frown as they opened up their

sacks and began to parcel out provisions and an old fur
tunic, which would make a warm blanket for a small per-
son. "We will come back," Arl said, presenting them to
her. "There are places here to hide among the rocks. You
will be safe. I promise we will return."

"Nome. I gowidyou," Snip said, and could not be
coaxed to stay.

Arl shrugged. "I suppose it makes no matter. Come here
then, Snippet. You shall ride on my shoulders awhile."

Fith and Cat hastily bundled up the small heap of sup-
plies and thrust them in a hollow among the boulders.
When they had filled the hollow up with stones, they hurried to come up to Arl.

At the head of the stony valley, the climbing Way bent
back to the right—north again, toward the mine, but far
above it. Or so Arl supposed, though for all his scouting
skill and Cat's wizardry at waycasting, neither of them
could have sworn so. It curved upward around the shoulder of one of the great peaks. They had not traveled far
enough south along the valley for it to be the topless fire
mountain Lek had pointed out from the pass above the
glacier, but the path was gritty with ash, and in some
places completely drifted over. Arl, in the lead still, had to
crouch gingerly and sweep it away with one hand. It
made for awkward and frightening going, for having
taken Snip upon his shoulders, Arl could not safely put
her down again. The Way was too narrow, even if it was
not the single paw's breadth of Findral's tales. As ash
slithered downward, Cat whispered to herself, "O Great
Mirel, let no one be a-watch below!"

After an hour they gained the safety of a place where
the Way became for a dozen yards or so a trench cut
through an outthrust spur of rock upon the mountain's

flank. Arl set the Ashkin's child down thankfully and leaned against the mountainside.

Fith folded up with a sigh, to sit on his heels with his arms clasped about his trembling knees. "Ho! It's no wonder Lek's not come this far yet. Is *all* the Wolf Way so dangerous?"

Snip's only reply was a blank look. Perhaps her folk did not count high, sheer precipices dangerous.

Cat rested her folded arms on the rough-cut parapet overlooking the misty valley and strained to see ahead. She could make out neither the ledge or walled mouth of the vindurn mine, or the smoke of the Rokarrhuk campfires. The valley curved like a misty moat at the mountains' feet, and the switchback in their trail apparently had not carried them far enough back along that curve to spy the Great Gate and the encampment before it. There seemed, at least, to be no pursuit. Yet though no creature stirred, some elusive thing in that stark and darkly beautiful landscape sounded a faint alarm. Cat frowned, but then the small doubt was swallowed in a greater one as she looked ahead along the trail.

"The path! It ends just there!" she cried.

Arl came to look. Several yards beyond where they stood, the parapet trailed off and the ledge narrowed once again, curving round the mountainside into the shadows of yet another cleft. But where before the path had always climbed out again, a thin, telltale line traced up the mountain's face, here it did not.

Alarmed, they gathered up their things and hurried on, fearful of what they might find. Only Snip seemed undismayed. She seemed, in fact, to be greatly pleased and ran ahead with a thin cry of "Dizzay! Urry-urry!"

The deep cleft that fell away on their right had once, they saw, been a stair of waterfalls spilling down into the great valley from a dark stream-mouth at the chasm's head. It was to that dark hole that their path led. No more than a trickle ran from it now, glistening down long falls of billowed stone that had been smoothed and swirled by a stream that was already ancient in the Times Before.

Snip scrambled up over the rocks at the path's end.

"Wait!" Arl called. "What is this place?"

"Woov'ay. You come an godroo moundop."

Cat, coming last, hunched down like the others at the low entrance but ended by going on her hands and knees, dragging her sack behind her. The roof lifted up into darkness after several yards, and in the dim light the Tiddi could see only that they were in a space larger than a water passage. Down its middle the ancient stream had shaped a gentle, sloping course out to the curved lip of its spillway. The old stream bed made a smooth and gentle footpath along each side of the narrow, deep-carved rivulet that ran there now.

Cat was uneasy. "I don't like it. And the oil and bit of candle we have left won't last an hour out."

But even as she spoke, the Ashkin's child took Arl's hand to guide it to a niche in the wall close by.

"Here are lamps!" Arl's hand brushed a jar nearby, and he unstoppered and sniffed it. "And oil. Almost half a bottle."

The lamp he lit burned with a small, smoky flame at first, owing to the dampness of the chamber and the clay lamp itself, but it was enough to show a wide niche, its shelf strewn with stone lamps—some whole, some broken, and all but a few crusted with grime. The small, guttering flame was echoed in the crystals that gleamed in narrow veins overhead and here and there along the walls. Cat's uneasiness deepened, but Arl's eyes were wide and dark, more with wonder than alarm.

Fith looked around eagerly. "What is it? Is this the

cavern in your dream? The way Olf and Oona brought you out from under the mountain?"

Arl shivered. "No, the stream there was more of a stream. And stone icicles hung from a roof far higher than this. The light from my mother's lamp could not touch it. And there were stairs. Besides, there we climbed down, not up—unless, of course, this way joins that other. But we never came out of Everdark by such a narrow, nasty path as what's behind us. I couldn't have forgotten that!"

"It's queer we've not met Lek yet," Fith said. "Unless, being the Wolf Way, there are other places like this stream's mouth too low for a Man. He would have to go on all fours. Or he might have run into t-trouble."

"Rokarrhuk or owl trouble? We'd best go warily ourselves," Arl said.

Cat scowled. "I mistrust this place. It feels—*wrong.*"

Arl tried to sound cheerful. "At least we shall sleep under cover instead of clinging to the mountain's face." Against his own misgivings he turned and padded after Snip, who waited impatiently at the lamplight's edge.

The caverns, though they were not so high or broad as the caves of Arl's dreams, were strange and wonderful. Everywhere were the ruined stumps of what once had been icicles and pillars of stone. Cut down like trees for the silky mottled rose or green or violet stone that hid beneath their crust of brownish gray, they showed that many miners once had worked there. The deep-gouged veins of milky crystals that glimmered on the roof and walls bore marks of ancient miners' chisels: blurred and softened marks left there deep in the mountain's past and glazed over by the age-long seep of water. In little mounds of dripstone everywhere, the mountain had set about the long rebuiding of its columns.

The companions traveled half a league in uneasy silence. Coming upon the dark pool that fed the trickling stream, they saw that though the old channel had poured down from a hole gaping far overhead, the water now was no more than a gathered seepage from the weeping walls.

Beside the pool the path veered away to the right, and they followed. Every moment they expected it to cease its steady climb, perhaps to end in some wind-scoured cave high on the outer rim of the Fennethelen, or to bend downward to rejoin the outer Wolf Way at some lower height. Instead, it climbed more steeply still until, unexpectedly, it ended at the foot of a long, narrow flight of stairs.

Stairs with short, much-worn steps. Stairs that might have been made to measure for a Tiddi foot, a Tiddi stride, but—for the Wolves of Aam?

The *pid-pad-pid-pad* of the child's feet faded up and away.

"Snip? *Snip!*"

There was not even a faint *pid-pad* for answer.

The three friends huddled at the narrow stair's foot.

"That," said Fith nervously, "is a stair to make even Findral Nimblepaw stumble. How can it be the Wolf Way?"

"It cannot." Arl gritted his teeth, and then sighed. "The little demon! She has led us out of our way, and it must be near nightfall outside. Lek will think us lost."

"Or taken by Rokarrhuk." Cat did not add, as she might have done, that for several leagues she had felt something to be wrong.

"Where *are* we then?" asked Fith.

Arl peered up the stair, but seemed reluctant to set foot on it. "I do not know. Wherever it is, I do not care for it."

Cat, remembering the shallow curve of the mist mountain valley far below their trail—*a curve*, she suddenly realized, *that bent the wrong way*—was suddenly very frightened, but she held her tongue. How could she have been so easily deceived? But perhaps she was mistaken. Even if she were not, there was no good to be had from alarming young Fith . . .

"I think we should go on," said Fith stoutly. "For a little way, at least—until we find a place where we can dance the Sun down. If the Fennethelen is honeycombed with mines, even if we have come wrong, this still *could* take us through the mountaintop to rejoin the old Wolf Way."

Curiosity warred with Arl's uneasiness. "Perhaps—but why has the child brought us this far, and then left us? . . . unless she has gone to fetch another of her folk. Of *my* folk . . ."

Cat, at the stair's foot, lifted her lamp high. "Then the sooner we see, the sooner we know."

Though steep, the stair proved short. The twentieth step was a narrow landing, but no door opened from it. If once there was one, it had been sealed up so craftily that no sign of it remained. Instead, hand- and footholds stepped up the wall's smooth face, and overhead a small, flattish opening barely large enough for a Tiddi to wriggle into pierced the wall.

"I shall go first." Arl's boldness could not quite hide his nervousness.

At the end of the hole he found himself on a low, broad ledge high above a corridor lined with stout dripstone pillars. Somewhere beyond, the bright light of a torch flickered and, blowing out his lamp, Arl signaled with a low whistle for the others to follow. When Fith and Cat were stretched out beside him, he snuffed out their lamps too.

"Why? What is—" Fith began, but a quick jab of Cat's elbow silenced him.

Through the screening pillars they could see a domed,

round room from which passageways branched in three directions. Cat felt Arl's shoulder tremble against her own.

"Why are you afeared?" she signed with her fingers on his wrist.

Arl's answering whisper was almost too faint to hear. "This place is no mine shaft in the Fennethelen. I know that room. I am sure of it. I—"

Cat's fingers tapped a warning on his shoulder. "Listen." *Pid-pad-pid-pid-pid pad-pad* . . .

Scarcely breathing, the friends watched as four small shadows detached themselves from the gloom far down the passage opposite and slipped along the wall.

Snip. Snip and three others older than herself, like her scantily dressed, but pale as mushrooms.

Abruptly the child stopped. She seemed for a long moment to be listening, and then all four turned at once to scurry back the way they had come.

Arl strained to hear what had alarmed them. Nothing. A full minute crept by before Fith, whose ears were sharpest, pointed urgently away to the left. A moment more and Arl, then Cat, heard the distant thud of marching feet. Rokarrhuk. Quickly they wriggled backward until they could see neither side corridor, and only a part of the chamber.

Round-headed, wide-shouldered, bandy-legged, beast-faced, sweating, clad in metal-studded leather tunics and armed with iron-knobbed truncheons, the Rokarrhuk soldiers hurried past at the double, disappearing way to the right. At the last echo of their passing, Arl scrambled out and over the ledge, dropping to the floor below, and peered cautiously between the pillars.

"Come," he signed to Cat and Fith, and darted across the open space into the central passageway where Snip and her companions had disappeared.

The three friends ran, hurrying past each torch in its

stone bracket and into the sheltering shadows beyond. Rounding a corner, they were brought up short by the sight, a short distance ahead, of six or seven Rokarrhuk soldiers lounging beside a heavy iron door in the left-hand wall. The three Tiddi stepped quickly backward and out of sight. Snip and the Ashkins had vanished, but where to?

Arl searched the shadows high on the wall. "There has to be a hiding place. Or a secret passage."

"There!" Fith pointed.

Cat, looking where he gestured, saw a small, pale, pointed face whisk out of sight, like a conjuror's trick, into the rock itself. The illusion was a simple one. A low opening like that through which they had entered the mountain halls was masked from below by a flange of rock that was invisible against the rough-hewn roof. Hand- and toe-holds in the wall were cunningly made to seem no more than broken places in the rock.

Cat first, then Fith, then Arl swung up and through the narrow opening, to squirm across a ledge like that behind the pillars in the round room and drop into the chamber beyond.

It was a large room, low roofed but wide, and lit by a score or so of lamps in niches on the walls.

And it was crowded with pale, fair-haired little creatures like the poor, dead Ashkin.

Tiddi. Hundreds of them.

11. ANOTHER WAY

In the valley beyond the Fennethelen, Lek stared through the midday gloom at the tall, thin figure striding across the glacier's ashen snow, following Findral. A large black bird circled overhead. "*Ollo?*" Lek exclaimed. "It cannot be. And Hlik with him!"

Findral, sitting on his haunches, grinned. "Indeed it is Ollo. Eating meat instead of moss helped, but it was recovering his wits that worked the transformation. Hlik sent us a visitor out of the West before he came himself. It was soon after you had gone. A strange, humpbacked Man. Ollo called him Flute. At least, I think he was a Man. The medicines he brought were as swift and sure as the old, true magic—much stronger than yours."

"Mnnn." Lek was only half attending.

The figure so rapidly approaching, though not so tall as Lek himself, was straight and sure of stride. Even the blowing folds of his gown and cloak, snapping in the wind, added to his commanding air. Under his close-fitting fur helmet's peak the Wizard's face was as youthful as his gait.

"Where are these Tiddi of yours?" demanded Ollo as he swept down from the ice onto the snow slope at the mountains' foot. "They must be hardy Tiddi indeed to fare so far from their endless chase after Astarlind's fine weather.

Where are they while you stand watch in this grim place? Snug in a snow cave, I warrant."

"They are gone. Vanished," Lek said in anguish. Turning away, he paced up and down as he told of the dead little Ashkin, of his hole, and of the hoped-for meeting with the Tiddi beyond the Fennethelen. Lek had found the Wolf Way and lost it again, for a great length of it near the crest had been cut away—deliberately. Rock-cutting tools had left their telltale marks. By the evening he had safely retraced his steps. Taking shelter by the rock that hid the Ashkin's hole, he had heard clearly, but from far off, a great din of hammering, of breaking rock and of harsh voices calling.

"That was the night before last. At dawn yesterday and again this morning a troop of owls came scouring down the ice river. Looking for me, I guessed, but twice luck sent a snow at nightfall to cover my tracks. If it had not, those great snowbirds would have led the Rokarrhuk to my snowdrift."

"Rokarrhuk. Hah!" Ollo skewered him with a sharp glance. "I have heard about those creatures from young Findral. And you have seen more of them. What I do not understand is by what road *they* pass in and out if the old Wolf Way is no more. Have you discovered it?"

"Yes, hidden at the head of a high, narrow valley some five leagues south of here. But much good knowing so will do us! It is a broad, rough-hewn tunnel driven straight through the mountain, set with great iron gates and windows in the canyon walls for sentinels. It is the work of the Naghar's folk, for it is too grim a place to have been fashioned by the Silvrin."

"Ah, um," said Ollo. "And you did not try to pass the gates? Did you not master the art of Transparencies before your Master's death?"

Lek shook his head, saying bitterly, "I am a master of

leading good friends into danger, but not of that art. When Master Azra died, my apprenticeship was only half accomplished, so I am not even a journeyman conjuror. It is a great day when I can make a mouse vanish."

"A pity. A great pity, for though there was once another way, haste is called for. Your Tiddi friends may be in graver danger than you fear. Mind you, I only guess. I have not seen Avel Timrel since I was a boy, and that was—some time ago. I meant to come here when wizards were banished from Umeár after the theft of the Nirim-stone. Abandoned or no, Avel Timrel would be a pleasant refuge for a student of the stars, I thought. But I heard evil rumors of the place: that it was taken over by owls and outlaws. Your news, as Findral tells it, makes me fear much worse."

"I do not fear it. I know it." Lek's gaze was bleak. "In the instant I spied the iron gate I knew that Avel Timrel had become Nagharot. When I was prisoner in Gzel the Captain there spoke of the Lord Naghar's owls—a grim jest about his being fed to them if he failed to recover the Moonstone. And the owls I have seen here do not fly south from the Owl Mountains, but across the Fenne-thelen's peaks from Avel-Timrel-that-was. Owls and Rokarrhuk together can only mean that the Shadowlands are Nagharot's. In my heart I must have known it could be so, but my mind was filled with the Opal Mountain and my dreams with a new Nirim, a new Worldstone for Umeár."

Ollo's dark brows fluttered up. "Blame yourself for your friends' predicament if you wish, but I fear you cannot take all the credit. There is something stranger here than a bandit lord who wishes to set himself up as King of the City of the Moon Under the Mountain. Too many threads draw together: your young friend Arl's dreams of 'Everdark'; the theft of Lisar the Sunstone and Nirim the Worldstone; the mystery of the fate of Tionel, the stone that once was kept in Aam; the spreading Shadows; and the attack on me. That was no chance thuggery, but a cunning ambush. Too cunning to have come from the minds of the Men who accomplished it."

He lifted his face to the mountain towering above them. "No, whether it is good fortune or ill that has drawn you here, I cannot say. Or whether it was chance or foredoom. Beyond the Fennethelen may lie Nagharot and Everdark and Melurath, the Mouth of Darkness of the Tiddi tales, but it is also the Opal Mountain, and Avel Timrel, City of the Moon Under the Mountain. And the name Fennethelen still means 'Spring's Stronghold.' "

"*And* there are still Silvrin in Astarlind," put in Findral, who saw no point in tasting despair before defeat. "Basadil's folk in the Farther West. Hlik has seen them. They may no longer rule it like princes, as in the old days of Aab and Avella and Aam's glory, but they are its guardians still, and powerful."

Ollo looked up to search the frowning sky for the great raven, and at last spied him far to the south. He raised a thin hand, and the tiny fleck that was great Hlik wheeled and sped toward them.

As Hlik swooped down to perch on Lek's strong shoulder, Findral, the lover of tales, suddenly sprang up. His ears thrust stiffly forward and his golden eyes glinted with excitement. "The Silvrin . . . Of course! I am a slow-wit for forgetting. The Wolves of Aam and the other elf-friends among the mortals came and went by Avel Timrel's Wolf Way, but the Silvrin and other Aldar did not. They '*marched out nine abreast, in silk and silver dressed, to fare into the West,*' the old Song says. So there *must* be another gate, another Way."

"There is," Ollo agreed. "Or was, and may be still. But only the Aldar could pass in by it. It lay eastward a good many leagues from here. But come!" He turned with a swirl of cloak and strode along the margin of the ice, calling back, "Let us hope your Tiddi friends can keep out of mischief for three or four days!"

12. THE MOUNTAIN FOLK

"Lobbers!" grumbled one in the crowd of Ashkins in the wide, low-ceilinged chamber. "Yan was a troublemaker, with 'is talk of zunzhine an green grazz, an now 'is brat brings uz Lobbers! How can we hide zuch lummoggy darkles?"

"Why zhould we? Zuch zoft-handed, loud-vooted, weak-eyed volk are no good vor miners. Two're too tall vor the opal workins een if they do know one end ovva mattick vrum nother."

"Karrugs'll gettem anyhow."

The murmur, like the hum in a hive of angry honey-bees, still thrummed in Arl's ears as he scrambled up the narrow passage of the airwell behind a young Ashkin.

"Why do you mistrust us? They called us 'Lobbers' as if they hated Lobb the Singer too, from long ago. Why?" whispered Fith.

"Zzzzzh!" The soft warning came from above and was followed by a small shower of gritty dust. "Zound travels var in airwells."

Avel Timrel's system of airshafts was almost as great a wonder as the glimpses the three Tiddi had, through vents, of halls and chambers that glowed like firelit gemstones: a corridor with polished walls of banded rose and beige and soft gray-green; a large, milky-gray hall with clustered columns of brown and green and brownish-purple opal, marvelously strange; and a small room like a hollow jewel, carved out of one great, shimmering honey-orange stone, its inner fire flickering opal-like with tongues of orange and cardinal red. The air shafts were dark and often rough walled (and a tight squeeze for Cat), but they twined and twisted, turned and climbed among the mountain's halls—a second, secret city within the City of the Moon Under the Mountain.

Arl felt a rough wall before him, and neatly cut toe-holds. He was about to follow the soft draught of air upwards when he felt a touch on his shoulder.

"Inneer."

A pair of firestones clicked somewhere close ahead, and then a small, glowing coal of fire was touched to a lamp-wick. The lamplight showed a low-ceilinged, wide chamber. As the Ashkin bringing up the rear crawled in, a rock was rolled across the entrance and another pulled away from a hole in the wall opposite. The air, uncomfortably warm in the passageways, grew fresh and cool.

"Thiz is our hiding hole. We gather mozz out on the mounzide," one of their guides said happily, "an dry it vor tinder. The olders dunno. They alluz keep the lamps, an light one vrum nother. They think without lamps youngles woan go var enough to ged into drouble."

The three Ashkins sat on their heels and regarded Arl and Cat and Fith shyly. The eldest of them, who was about Arl's age, held Snip close. Milky pale like most of their folk, with long, tied-back hair the color of new-cut ashwood, they shared with Snip a liveliness that made them seem more truly Tiddi than their furtive, timid kin-folk. Their soft, murmuring speech was harder to hear than to understand.

"You call Eenilla Znip? It vits. Znip!" The eldest

grinned, but then said with Tiddish formality, "We are Znip's ungles. I am Bort, an these are Zdil an Gelly. You zay our brother Yan is dead, zo now we muz care vor er. An we'll help you iv we can, vor you brought er zafe back vrum the Dark Cold World."

"An you can tell uz all about the Dark Cold World," put in Gelly eagerly.

Zdil, the middle brother, said shyly, "Our brother Yan, ee zaid the Zhadow dint go on forever—maybe ony a lil ways. The olders zaid ee was crazy. Znip's mother was ztolen away vor the Danze, an Yan zaid ee had to take Znip zafe away vrum Everdark, zhe was zo lively—a zparkle, like er mother. Darkle an zparkle, zhe'd vor sure be taken vor a Zhadow Danzer, an we would never zee er again. Zo they went. An now ee's vrozen, poor Yan!"

Snip and her uncles went, leaving the three friends in the hiding hole and promising to return in the morning well before the Rokarrhuk came to herd their Ashkin slaves down into the mines. It was too late to dance the sun down or the Moon up, and so the travelers curled up together, and slept.

For Arl, sleep came slowly. The Dance . . . The questions that had clamored in his mind on the long crawl up through the airwells were stilled, and he lay in a half-dream of long ago, and two soft voices. *"But Arl—he's our only! He muzt not go to the Danze! The Naghar always takes the darkles. Because they are like the Old Volk, my vather zays." "Aye, but he cannot live all is life in the airwells like Ruz an Zula. We can paint im . . ." "No! We muzt not! Zooner nor later the painted ones always pine away. No, we'll vind Melurath, or Doril's Hole, an go out into the Dark, Cold World. The Zhadows can't go on vorever . . ."*

Arl slept, though it seemed that only moments passed

before he heard Fith's eager morning chatter and murmured Ashkin answers beyond the edge of that same dream. Sleep still held him, and the half-heard voices lapped against his dreams of childhood.

Gelly's eyes were round, and bright with lamplight. "An Lisar the Zun ztill zhines?"

"A-courze it does," scoffed Zdil. "Didden Yan zay zo? An you've been out mozz gathering—you've *zeen*. How elze would noon zhadows be lighter than night zhadows?"

Bort was doubtful. "Vordibee the Wise zays it is because the Naghar's meddling with the vire-mountain lights a great beacon in the zky."

"I don't know about that," Fith said, "but Arrn the Sorcerer stole the Sunstone, not the Sun. There's still a Sun. And sunshine, only twelve days' journey beyond the Fennethelen. The sooner we head for it, the better. All of us. All of *you*. Our friend cannot go opal-hunting in a mountain full of Rokarrhuk, so not even he will wish to stay."

Snip's ears pricked up at this welcome news, but her uncles drew together in alarm.

"Go? But we haven't vinished the Mountain! There's ztone to be worked and ztones to be mined. Crystals to be zet, and columns polizhed! Where would we vind another zo beautivul to work in?"

"But . . ." A puzzled Cat spoke for Fith as well. "You are Tiddi too, and Tiddi are wanderers—hunters as well as craftsmen. You would be free to follow the Wandering Way again."

"Wandringay—what iz that?"

Fith was shocked. "Don't you know the Star Circle Song? The Wandering Way is the path from one Song circle to the next. The Wanderpath follows the Sun's circle as if it were drawn on the face of Astarlind: from Aam at Midsummer to Eem and Tha, and south to Aye at Midwinter. In Norimoon we turn north again through Saan and Min. Lobb searched out the Way after he led our forefolk out of Melurath."

Bort snorted. "Lobb! Ay, your prezious Lobb an his Lobbers vound Melurath. Vound an lozt it. It has not been vound again thiz long Age zince they pazzed through it out of Everdark."

"Melurath?"

Arl, still dazed with sleep, sat up, caught by the name, an echo of his dream. "Melurath . . . of course! All our riddles have one answer! This mountain has as many names as there are tongues: Avel Timrel, Everdark, Uval Garath, Melurath, your 'Beautivul Moun' and Nag-harot..."

"Na, Melurath is no name vor Everdark," Gelly, the youngest, objected. "It is the Hidden Door's name— 'Mouth of Darkness'—an one day I zhall vind it!"

Bort sighed. "Ai, ya! An if you do, who will go through it? You? I dint zee you or Zdil here go with Yan an his Eenilla avter ee opened up the old wrigglehole."

Gelly shrugged. "We're no Lobbers to go off an leave our olders when they won't go. Yan, ee had a zparkle-darkle child. Thazz divverent. Zparkles an darkles, they're vor the Danze. Ee had to get Eenilla—Znip—away."

"What are sparkles? And what Dance?" asked Fith.

"Juzt . . . the Danze." Zdil shivered. "There's alluz been the Danze. Zumtimes we hear the music in the airwells, very var away, an the youngles zing a Zong the olders zay is old as old:

> *Ring aroun the Day's Eye,*
> *Wrong way roun the Zun.*
> *Danze a net vor Lizar,*
> *An the dark has won.*

107

What it means, nobody knows, but old Vordibee, ee zays is great-grammer zang it too, an called the Danze a 'dark-zpell.' "

"It's alluz the darkles get taken," Bort explained as he knelt and open a lidded stone box he had brought with him. "Ever once in a while there's a darkle born—dark like you, like the Olden Volk in the Times Bevore. A darkle muzt pale imzelf with powdered ztone an paint to be zafe vrum the danzmazters' whips, or live always in the air-wells. A zparkle child is worse. It has a nose vor mischief, an ardly ever zleeps. Zum grow out of it. Like Gelly," he said with a grin. "But een then they dream of doors an mines an wriggleholes with zunzhine at the other end."

"Ai," Gelly said. "But I'd be avraid to go by my lone, or with only one or two. The Karrugs have long whips, an zpies that zee in the dark. Owls. Cruel owls." He sat back on his heels and dipped a brush into the paint pot Bort passed to him.

Some twenty silent minutes later, Fith, his chin held firmly by the paintbrush-wielding Gelly, slid his gaze idly to the right and smiled to see Arl's newly pale face and wide, wondering stare. Then he saw the astonishing sight Arl stared at: Cat, her hair stone-powdered to a pale, ashen gold, sitting still and cross-legged like an ivory queen, her thick-lashed eyes darker than ever against a skin like milky opal. Bort was closing up his paint box.

Fith gaped. "You look like the carving of Queen Teela in the tomb at Aam!"

Bort scowled. "Zhe won't do. Zhe looks no more like one of uz than beryl lookz like jade. Zuch ztrange eyes! You muzt keep them cazt down, Prinzess! Ztay away vrum lampz an torches, an take care the Karrugs doan zee you close-to. An ztoop. Are many of you darkle Lobbers zo tall?"

"Not many," said Arl before Cat could answer. He had meant to hold his tongue about his dream until he knew more about these odd, new-found kin, but now he leaned forward intently. "Did Olf and Oona—Did they leave Everdark because they had a darkle child they meant to keep from this Dance you talk of?"

Snip's uncles stared.

"How do you know *that*?" Bort whispered.

"Arl? Oona's Arl?"

Vordibee the Wise was a gnarled, shrunken little creature in a long leather tunic stamped all over with a design of overlapping feathers, each feather-tip rubbed with opal dust to glisten blue and green. Grasping the stone arms of his chair, the one high-backed seat among the benches carved for the olders around the walls, he sat up as straight as—being bent with age—he could.

"*Our* Oona's Arl? My ztars! Which of em is ee?"

The nearest Ashkins heard and craned to see, then whispered excitedly to their neighbors, "Oona's Arl!" until the news had rippled across the gloomy chamber to the farthest olders on their gleaming benches. In its wake came a surge of murmurings.

"*Oona's Arl? Not dead?*"

"*An come here with Lobbers? What can it mean?*"

"*Tizzen true! Kappen Koorg zaid they tracked em east away. Zaid they killed em.*"

"*Fa, all Iggans an Karrugs're liars, arn they?*"

"*Trouble, thaz what it means. Lobb was trouble, Lobbers're trouble.*"

This was too much for Fith. He glared at the sea of pale, curious eyes and then turned indignantly to face old Vordibee.

"If you are chief here, tell them to hold their tongues.

Lobb the Singer was the greatest Tiddi of all. Even if he were not, he died an Age ago—how can they hate him still?"

"Why? Because ee ztole our Zongs an our hopes away," snapped the old Tiddi. "When the Naghar virst came, Lobb was Zinger, an ee knew the zecret Zong of Melurath, an wished to lead all the volk out by that way. An when the olders an the Makers an the volk with the littlest children dint wish to leave the Beautivul Moun, an bade im wait to learn if all the Naghar's promizes be true, did ee? No, ee took is harp an cap an all our bravest youngles. Harped um out vrum under the mountain in the middlenight, een though the King had vorbid their going. An the zecret of Melurath went with um."

Fith was glad for the painted mask that hid his flush. "But—t-to hate him s-*still* . . ." he protested. Even as he spoke, he knew that if he could feel shamed by so long-ago a deed, the Ashkins still could feel betrayed.

"Ah, but you doan really zee! Ee was Zinger, wunt ee?" Old Vordibee spoke more gently, seeing Fith's distress. "The youngle ee was teaching to be Zinger avter im went too, an between em they took away all the Tales an Zongs an Legends packed up in their heads, dint they? Ever zince, we've had no more than the bones an zcraps their olders could ztitch together. With our Lists an Zongs to give us heart, our volk might ztill have been prisoners in the Beautivul Moun, but never zlaves."

Fith nodded dumbly. For Tiddi such a loss was beyond measuring. He could not imagine life without its Songs and Tales, and was relieved when Vordibee the Wise turned to peer at Arl.

"Zo, young Arl. You have come vull circle."

"I did not mean to, but I have," Arl said ruefully as he bowed. His painted cheeks were too stiff for smiling. "It was kindly done to send Bort and Gelly and Zdil to bring us clothing and new skins, but we do not mean to stay. We must find our traveling companion and warn him away from the Mountain. As soon as the way is clear, we will go the way we came."

"Ai, ya!" Old Vordibee beamed and nodded, seeming much relieved. "Indeed, as zoon as it is zafe. But now you muzt zhare our mornmeal. Go now, with Bort, like good childern." He shooed them away with a little flapping motion of his long fingers. The eager, listening crowd, a sea of pale eyes, parted and then closed in again behind the three friends.

Cat, a full head and a half taller than the mountain Tiddi, looked back across their heads and saw a ring of excited olders huddled close around Vordibee's chair, leaving the benches empty of all but one darker-skinned, old creature, almost invisible in a cloak of gray owl feathers, who sat dull-eyed and motionless at the furthest end of the olders' bench, staring vacantly at the shadowy ceiling. Cat frowned, but then her ears pricked up and the moment of uneasiness was forgotten as she heard Fith's clear, high voice begin the Sunrise Song:

> *O rim of gold*
> *Who peered of old*
> *Above the hill of Pilipold,*
> *Come glimmer at us*
> *dancing here . . .*

"Zoftly, zoftly!" someone warned.

Cat smiled to see a small bulge above the waist of Fith's tunic give a wriggle. The skimpy Ashkin garment fit too snugly for Tootoo's comfort. None of the mountain folk

seemed to notice the movement, for they were caught in
the silver snare of Fith's clear, thin chant.

> O arc of gold
> Who rose of old
> And chid the cold
> Away from Tidd . . .

While he sang, Fith moved slowy into the circle of the
Dawn's Dance. At this the mountain folk drew back a
little in alarm and whispered among themselves. "The
Danze . . . Izzit the Danze?" As they did so, Fith, singing
all the while, reached down the neck of his tunic and—as
matter-of-factly, as if he did not know the Ashkins had
good reason to mistrust owls, produced Tootoo and set
her on his shoulder. At first the Ashkins closest to him
flinched back a little, but then the circling Dance and
Song held them still—and Tootoo was very small, so small
that she looked more like a child's feathered toy than a
proper owl.

> O wheel of gold
> Who rolled of old
> Above green Yold—
> Too long you've hid!
> Come shine upon us dancing here.

At the Song's end the great room filled with an excited
buzz. The sullen stares were gone.
"Is the Zun *really* like a bowl of gold?"
"An it zhines even in the winter?"
"I tell you, *tiz* an owl."
"Tizzen!"
"Tiz a lovely Zong! Nabb knows the virst bit, but ee

zings 'Above the bell that Lilla tolled,' and that dunt make zense."

"No more danzing, though, young Lobber," one said. "Tizzen safe. The Karrugs have zpy-holes by the door. It is not zafe to know how to danze."

"Zing the Zong again," several urged. They thrust forward a short, white-haired Tiddi more sleek and plump than his fellows. "Teach it to Nabb. Ee's our Zinger, een if all he knows are zcraps."

"Na, na!" Nabb held up a pudgy hand. "We've no use vor zunrises here, nor moonzets. But—the Lizts, now! Do you know any of the Lizts?"

"Or Tales?" Gelly put in excitedly. "Zing uz a Tale!"

Fith was driven back against the wall by the eager crowd. "Yes!" He laughed. "I know some of the Lists and Legends, and many of the Tales. My mother is Queen, but I would rather be Singer-of-Tales than King, and so our Singer teaches me."

"Ai, hah!" the Ashkins cried, forgetting caution in their delight. "Ai, hah! vor Vith the Talebearer!"

A sudden low-pitched warning whistle from Vordibee quelled the excitement as water quenches fire. Bort, breathless and dusty, came thrusting through the crowd.

"The wrigglehole! They vound it! The Karrugs're zealing it up, an Cappen Koorg an the work guards're coming this way."

"Zo early? Quick, then!"

In a moment mornmeal kettles vanished under benches, the last sack of mushrooms was shared out, and lamps were snuffed and hidden away. When the heavy stone door rumbled open, torchlight spilled in across a pale tangle of Tiddi: some huddled together in families, others sprawled or stretching as if they waked from sleep, dull-eyed and sullen.

"Up, maggots!"

The harsh command that followed on the whip's crack was low, but every Ashkin scrambled up to stand like a spellbound mouse fixed by an adder's stare. Arl hung his head to hide his dark eyes, but chanced a sideways glance at the Rokarrhuk captain. His heart quailed.

Captain Koorg was no Rokarrhuk. Tall, green-gowned, Man-straight, he scanned the room with round, yellow beast's eyes. Cat, crouched close by, saw him in the same moment, and Arl heard her soft hiss of alarm.

The Illigan. The Captain of Gzel. And not dead. Not dead at all.

13. THE SHADOW DANCERS

"BUT HE *was* DEAD," Cat hissed as Rokarrhuk guards began sorting the Ashkins into gangs of miners and stonecrafters. "I saw him dead."

Certainly the alarming figure who strode to the head of the wide column of miners was the image of the dreaded Illigan: the same large, rounded ears, high-set on the round skull; the long, broad nose and short upper lip; the short, silky hair that grew alike on skull, brow, cheek and chin, as on a beast . . . and the tail that twitched below the green gown's hem.

" 'Iggans.' Gelly said something about 'Iggans and Karrugs,' " Fith whispered. " 'Iggans' must be Illigans. Why shouldn't there be more than one?"

Arl had no chance to answer, for four Rokarrhuk came stumping along the benches, driving the laggards into their work groups. "You, there in the shadows!" one shouted, cracking his whip. "Into line, skulker!"

Cat scrambled backward into the darkness of the high, hidden airwell just as Nabb the Singer popped up at Fith's elbow to urge him into the line of stonecrafters as they moved into the passage.

With a parting gesture to Fith that was the hunters' sign for "Be wary," Arl fell in among the miners and worked his way into their midst. *Think of nothing but this moment, this place,* he warned himself. If the Illigan of Gzel could hear the mind's speech and listen to dreams, so, he guessed, could this Illigan.

There was much to be seen and marveled at on the long way down to the opal workings among the mountain's roots. The torchlit passages and stairways—in the higher levels sometimes straight-cut with rich and curious carving in the colored stone, then, more frequently, the winding beds of vanished streams down dripstone-curtained corridors or through groves of fantastic columns —passed many halls and chambers. Marvelous opal chambers such as those they had seen from the airwells soon gave way to splendid halls at once cavernous and more cavelike. Often the stream of hurrying miners that filled the passage passed doorways that opened into honeycombs of smaller rooms or echoing unlit, unused caverns. Avel Timrel had indeed been a great city, but its works were drifted deep in dust. And where did the Lord Naghar live? Where were the Rokarrhuk quartered? Where in all this wilderness of rooms did the Tiddi craftsmen work, and at what? Why—

With an effort Arl wrenched his thoughts away from such restless questions and fixed his mind upon the route along which the long-limbed Illigan led the miners. They traveled at least a league, passing through a circular hall with a great, crystal-studded central column, out of which six passages radiated. From this Arl judged that they were somewhere near the mountain's center and marked in his mind the passageway by which they had entered. After that came more wonders still: a passage filled with crystal-frosted icicles of stone, a long, broad stair turning downward to the right, and a series of long chambers where the walls were lined with great domed ovens that looked like the mud nests of giant dauberbirds turned upside-down. Down the center of each kitchen marched a third row of ovens. Such kitchens must have been meant to feed the whole of a city greater even than Arl had been imagining! In each, a high, central vent hole in the vaulted, smoke-darkened ceiling looked like a far-off black hole in a moonless night sky.

Arl shivered. Only when his glance touched in passing on the Illigan, scant yards ahead, did he remember Bort's warning to keep his eyes down. So much to see, and he must not look! Unless . . .

In the first great kitchen, when the stream of mountain folk divided to pass down both sides of the central row of ovens, he had noticed that the open mouth of the first oven faced the door by which they had entered. After that, one oven faced right, the next one left, alternating down the row. The second kitchen followed the same practical arrangement. There he saw that, as he hoped, the last oven faced the archway into the third kitchen.

Moving forward unnoticed, in the stream of miners, Arl soon put himself ahead of all but two of the Rokarrhuk soldiers. The two ahead trotted heavily behind the strid-ing Illigan and, like their captain, never bothered to look behind. Why should they? The Ashkins were well trained. Even in the wide world, Tiddi did not like change, prefer-ring each day, each year to be much like the last, and long years of servitude had left the mountain folk more timid still. They ran jerkily, like mice the cat has dazed, and their eyes were dull.

Working his way leftward across the jostling crowd of miners, Arl came abreast of the last of all the ovens and brushed close against it. While his neighbors swept on past, he slipped around to the front and sprang up and into the oven.

The smoke-dark, shadow-filled oven had little head-room, but was wider and deeper than he had supposed. Stretching out in the dust along the rear wall, he hoped that his new, pale skin would not betray him. The shadows were deep and the opening small, but . . . No, he must not think such things. He must not *think*.

The Illigan paused on the far threshold and cast a cold look back along the ragged column. Arl squeezed his eyes tight shut for fear the Illigan would feel the very touch of his gaze. Even when it seemed he must be safely gone, Arl did not look. He lay still and listened to the rustling, whispery *pid-pad* of many feet hurrying deeper into the mountain, and the spiteful *snack!* of whips snapping at laggard heels.

When at last he slid over the oven's lip to the floor, he almost slipped, and discovered that he was trembling with relief. Cautiously he inched his way along until he could peer around the oven's side, darting a quick look down the kitchen's length to make sure there were no Rokarrhuk stragglers.

Scouting the other side in the same fashion, Arl hurried back the way the column had come, keeping to the ovens' shadows. The kitchens were only dimly lit, but in his pale, painted skin he felt he must stand out like a hairy ammut on a snowfield.

There was much to marvel at—a painted frieze high along the walls, fire pits with spits large enough to roast a full-grown oorus—but Arl hurried past, for nothing seemed familiar to him. Somewhere in the mountain's warren lay the path he knew from his dreams, and he meant to find it. The sooner he and Fith and Cat were out and away, the better. The obedient, scuffling mountain folk frightened him. The floor along the wall ovens was paved with colored stone, but a wide swath along each

side of the central ovens and on along the miners' path .
was worn deep into the dark understone. Arl shivered to
think of so many generations of hurried feet, and the
thought sped his own.

If Olf and Oona did not escape through Doril's Hole,
what other way was there but Melurath? Issa's folk had
found small Arl and his slain parents at Eem, and Eem lay
to the south and east, beyond the Blue Mountains. Surely,
then, Melurath must lie on the mountain's eastern side.
But which way was east? And what of the Fennethelen?
It ringed the City, and Findral's Songs told of no way
for mortals to cross its jagged hedge of peaks but by the
Wolf Way . . .

Still, there was an answer, and if his father had found
it, he could.

Beside the foot of the broad stair curving up out of the
first kitchen, a narrow archway led to a second, down-
ward-curving stair. It was dusty and apparently little
used, but there were footprints enough to mask his own
long-toed ones so long as he kept to the wide end of each
tread. After more than a hundred steps, he began to wonder whether he might not do better to climb back up and
try some other way, but then he spied a faint light below
and kept on. Reaching its source after two hundred more
steps, he found only a broad landing above another curving flight, and the stump of a torch guttering in its socket.

Another flight! The City was worse than Gzel for stairs!
He sat for a moment on the landing and waited for his
knees to stop their weary trembling. After a moment he
pricked up his ears. A faint, thin thread of sound wound
up from below, almost too slight to hear.

A song? The strange, sliding melody was dimly familiar, but it had no sound of words to it. It was no harp,

but some instrument that caught the music of the wind. Perhaps it was no more than that: the wind singing in a corridor, in an airwell.

The second stair was shorter than he had judged: no more than thirty steps. The eerie music was muffled by the stout wooden door at the bottom. Arl set his shoulder to it and gave a cautious shove. It was heavy and twice as tall as he was, but to his surprise it swung open easily. At that moment the eerie music stopped, and a harsh voice crackled in its place.

Arl found himself in a gloomy, curving gallery separated from the central room it encircled by translucent stone draperies that hung in long swags and billows to the floor, as if they had been frozen by a magic breeze. The gallery's outer walls were hung with broken folds of delicate dripstone like tattered curtains that might crumble at a touch. Wavy ridges on the ceiling showed that once they had hung thickly, fold on fold, but these had been broken off to clear the ten or twelve-foot wide gallery passage and their edges smoothed. The dim light in the gallery came from the bright room just beyond, shining through the stone's rippled rose and gold.

At the sound of a whip's crack the untuned music piped up again, and a towering shadow-figure swayed across the golden screen.

Arl gasped—a little sound, half squeak, half sob. Tugging frantically at the ring handle on the heavy door, he pulled it shut and stood shivering in the stairwell's darkness. The torch had guttered out.

A shadow like a top-heavy, long-legged bird, awkwardly graceful . . .

The Shadow Dancers of his old dream!

14. EXPLORATIONS

How old had he been? Two years? Three? Why should a shadow moving in a simple Circle Dance seem so fearful a thing?

The memory slept too deep for waking, and the images that flickered in Arl's dreams were only fragments, but they were no less frightening for that. It seemed to Arl as he huddled on the dark stair that, just as the Dancing Room lay at the mountain's heart, the Shadow Dance lay at the heart of the darkness gathered over Avel Timrel, the old heart of Astarlind. The why of it he could not fathom, except that it had something to do with his old dreamstone, the stone Mirelidar, safe now in an Iceling house under the Deep Ice at Werrick. Safe from the Naghar, who called it his own.

Arl reached for Lek's stone on its cord for the comfort of its warmth, and then remembered that he had given the stone to Cat for safe-keeping.

Suddenly, with no warning, the memory came flooding back, drowning the darkness and the cold stone step in pleasure . . .

Olf and Oona sat side by side on a wide windowsill, silhouettes against a gray day and dark peaks across a shadowed valley. The peaks were the spires of the

Fennethelen. He saw that now, but had not known it then. His parents' seat was the deep ledge of a natural window that opened out under a broad shelf of rock. *Watchful, listening, they rested. They had—they had passed through some great danger.*

Arl played in the shallow stream, swift and warm and wide, that plunged with a roar into the cavern at one end and vanished at the other. A fish, pale and goggle-eyed, slid across his foot. He laughed. He had called, "Here, vish!" and splashed after it. But it flicked out of sight. Grieved, he plumped down in the frothy water to wait for another.

As he paddled, a pale gleam in a shadowy pool under an overhang of rock caught his eye. "Vish!" This time it did not dart away at his splashing, but waited for him, rippling its pale rainbow scales.

It had been no fish, but the Moonstone, Mirelidar, lost for nine times ninety years. Oona had known it at once, and in her joy joined hands with Olf to dance a splashy circle around the stone-enchanted Arl. They did not dance for long. With the discovery of Mirelidar, long ago stolen from the Naghar and longer ago still from Basadil, the Silvrin King of Avel Timrel at the end of the Times Before, their escape was even more important. "Now we must travel day and night until we are safe away," Olf had said.

"Until we are safe away." The road to Melurath, the Mouth of Darkness, must have led through that low cavern with the window and the waterfall, but where was the cavern, which the stream?

In the upper city, the stoneworkers separated, each going to his own task. Nabb beckoned, but Fith hung back, keeping to the shadowed archway of the passage. He peered nervously into the long, oval room.

122

"What is this place?"

In some way he could not put a name to, the low-ceilinged hall was more unsettling than its anteroom, a chamber with lifelike stone dragons for sentinels and stone serpents writhing on the ceiling. Here too what must once have been a natural cavern was enlarged and utterly transformed. In other, lower, chambers the mountain's ribs and pillars were cunningly smoothed and polished to show the stone's best beauty or to shape it to a larger harmony, but here—here was a palace hall richer than any the Tales told of in ancient Aam or long-ruined Avella.

The ceiling, a low, long oval dome hollowed from the living rock, was the deep blue of a night-velvet sky crowded with stars that were flakes and crystals of pale yellow. The two long, curving walls of the same flecked, dark stone could scarce be seen for the hundred crowding pillars lined along them. At the room's far end the last pair—black, with thin mottled bands of shimmering blue-green—flanked a wide, low window shuttered against the outside weather. The floor was inset with stones of many colors, woven in a pattern so intricate and serpentine that Fith was half afraid to step upon it for fear it might writhe underfoot.

"Come in, come in!" Nabb the Singer said. "No Karrugs here in the Pillar Hall. They ztay outzide the door. Orders." He rubbed his hands and looked about him with pleasure, then motioned to the four master stone-workers who came behind. Two pushed at the great door until it stood barely ajar. The others fetched tools from a battered box nearby.

Nabb indicated a stepped dais two-thirds of the way toward the window, and the shallow pit that lay before it. "A little work there, and all is vanished. Zeven years work. All the bezt. It is zplendid, na?"

"Splendid," Fith said truthfully. He was a little dizzied by so much and such frantic splendor.

"The room is new-cut. Vrom all one zeam of porphyry," Nabb said proudly. "Many of the pillar ztones were brought vrom Gzel an Harju an the Indigoes."

"What is it all *for*?" Fith moved along the line of pillars, rose and blue and rust and gold. Even the most richly veined were carved in ringed or grooved or twisted shapes, or laced with graven patterns. "Who is it for? The old Nagger?"

"Zzzzh!" Nabb cast a nervous look over his shoulder. Taking Fith by the elbow, he drew him down the long room, away from the door. "Who elze would zuch a room be vor? Only mazter ztoneworkers have touched it. Today I zent Rew with the miners zo that you may come in his plaze an teach me vrom the Zongs an Legends while I work. We muzt vinish by Tinnimoon Eve, an that is only days away. Zee, the throne!"

Nabb, his eyes aglow with pride, swept a pudgy arm toward the massive high-backed seat of gleaming black that topped the dais. "Do you zee, we are zetting the gems around its base in the order vrom the Lizt of Ztones, vrom *Aa* to *Zozit*. The throne itzelf is Aa the Virestone, an here is Almandy, that zhines in dark, Amthiz, Beryl to work foes ill, Chrysopras . . ."

Fith, who did not fancy hearing all the hundred stones through to Zirco, Zois and Zozit, blurted out, "Have you seen the Nagger—the Lord Naghar? What is he? An Illigan? He can't be a Man if he's lived here ever since Lobb's day. Whatever he is, he must be a sorcerer. This looks like a sorcerer's hall!"

For all his pale color, Nabb went paler still. "We do not zee im. We do not think of im." After a moment, he added, "Ee goes away. Zometimes vor years, I think. The Karrugs grow lazy, but when he returns, they are avraid, an turn their whipz on uz." He would say nothing more. From a tool box beside the dais he handed Fith a stone pot and soft leather rag.

"Look around if you muzt, but quickly. The pot is polish. If the Karrugs open the door, you muzt zeem to polish dull zpots we have mizzed," Nabb said, adding, "There are none, of courze, zo make believe."

Fith moved to the low ledge under the wide, shuttered window, and under cover of opening his pot looked and found that the shutters had no chink or crack to show what lay beyond. Cloud, most likely. The stoneworkers had climbed many long ramps and stairs to reach these new rooms.

Rag in hand, he trailed along the pillared wall, trying to look as if he examined surfaces for flaws. Midway down the chamber he saw a shadow of a seam in the crystal-flecked blue wall that betrayed a narrow, high-arched door, concealed between two pillars, standing faintly ajar. One light, curious touch, and it snicked invisibly shut. His fingers could not even find the vanished seam.

Once or twice Fith fancied he was being watched and darted nervous looks behind him, in the direction of the door to the room of the stone dragons, but he met no spying eyes. It was his own reflection that drew him on to the last but one of all the pillars, a glistening black obsidian. Of them all, only this pillar of dark mirrorstone was plain of shape and bore no ornate carving. The wavy markings of its foot and crown were striations in the glass itself.

Standing before the pillar, Fith saw reflected in its wavy polished surface a spindly, crooked little creature and hardly knew it for himself until he remembered his painted skin. With a shiver he turned toward the sunken circle before the dais and its throne.

The sense of being watched had deepened. Fith made a

show of spying a scratch upon the lower step of the dais and rubbed at it industriously. His tour around the room had aimed for the crystal pedestal at the center of the sunken circle, but he did not want Nabb to know that. The Singer seemed only to care for his Songs and his handiwork, but something in his manner stirred Fith's hunter's caution, and so he had stalked the pedestal and the wide, crystal-lidded bowl atop it much as he would have crept up on a nervous elope.

It was a disappointment. The domed lid of the bowl hid no smoky mirror like the one that had snared Lek and almost caught Arl in Gzel before the fall of that grim stronghold. The bowl beneath held only an empty polished tray, an odd tray set with shallow cupped hollows.

Cat, in the confusion of pushing and stumbling as the miners and stoneworkers hurried into their work lines, had gained the safety of the airwell and watched and waited. When the heavy door slammed shut, she slipped down again to prowl the empty chamber—and found the odd, shrunken little Ashkin in the owl-feathered cloak. The older's empty gaze wandered over the ceiling, and when Cat spoke, she seemed not to hear.

"Are you ill?" Cat knelt beside her. "Do you want food? A cup of water?"

There was no answer.

"Shall I dance for you? The Dance of the Makers?"

Cat reached out to touch the small hand that trembled under the cloak's folds, but fell backwards as the tiny figure leaped up like a startled bird and fled across the sandy floor to cower in the farthest corner.

Shall I dance for you—was it so frightening a question? *Only to a Dancer come back from this Shadow Dance they speak of,* whispered Cat's heart, and she was frightened as she had not been even by the Illigan Koorg. Was coming back from the Dance as dreadful as vanishing, then? Most, they said, vanished.

Cat could not bear to stay and cause terror for so sad a creature. No more could she bear the thought of long hours in the hiding hole. But—if there were half as many leagues of airwells as of passages . . .

Tap-tap, tip-tap . . .

Cat, her ears pricked forward, crouched at a crossways where five airwells met and tried to sort out the faint *tip-tap* from its echoes. Tootoo, left hidden under a bench when Fith was swept away in the ranks of the stone-workers, was perched on her shoulder. The little owl appeared to like being thrust safely out of the way no more than did Cat herself. When she left the Ashkin quarters, Tootoo made for the airwell after her.

At one point in their explorations a whiff of cooler air, carrying with it a pungent smell, had drawn Cat down a narrow, sloping shaft to a grated opening that looked down into a long, shadowy room dimly lit by an arched window at its far end that opened onto gray daylight. Even as she watched, a great gray owl appeared upon the stone sill and, with a great flutter of wings, entered and sought out a perch among the long rows of roosts and drowsing owls. The chamber was an Owlery, for clearly the Naghar kept owls much as the old Kings in the Tales kept hawks. Small Tootoo, owl or no, trembled to see them and edged along Cat's shoulder to shelter among her dusty curls. She had not left her perch there even after Cat regained the main airwell.

Tip-tap-tap-t-tap.

The sound seemed to come from the second passage on the right, curving upward toward the mountain's western wall. Since the discovery that they had confused their direction in the valley's mist, Cat had made a point of

noting every turning, however slight, and tried to think of
the mountain's maze of layered passages as if she could
see them from above: a network like the trails of a much-
traveled woodland where the dabby's path crisscrossed
the deer's, the Tiddi way cut across the piggar track, and
the rabbit's scuttlings wound in and out among them all.
Few could best Cat at waycasting. Tootoo's courage returned and she fluttered eagerly ahead.

The *tip-tap* was closer now and clearer, ringing along
the stony walls. As Cat squeezed around a sharp bend, she
saw not far ahead a faint glow of light, and beyond it
another.

The first came from a short downward branch of the
airwell. She crept along it to its end, where an opening
gave a view down across a circular room through a thicket
of scaffolding to a high door flanked by ruby-eyed stone
dragons. Tiddi stoneworkers were everywhere, tip-
tapping, grinding, and polishing. One, at work high up
near the airwell setting fiery garnet eyes in a stone icicle
carved in the shape of a coiled snake, gave a squeak of
alarm as his eye met Cat's. Looking quickly away, he
began a shaky whistling that earned him a shout from one
of the Rokarrhuk prowling below.

Cat grinned and scrambled backward up the narrow
passage—not an easy feat.

At the bottom of a second dimly lit side shaft further
along the main passage she found not the usual hole
masked from viewers below only by an upward-tilted
ledge, but by a stone screen that was pierced with several
large and many small holes. Tootoo fluttered to the largest
hole, and Cat snatched her back just in time to prevent
her swooping down to join Fith, at work at Nabb the
Singer's side in a great, cavernous chamber. The half-
whispered strains of *Kyth on his lone, under Timmeril
Hill, Stone-finder, gem-shaper, tamer of Krill* . . . floated

up, a silken thread of song. No guards were in sight, but better to be safe than Tootoo-less. Also, Cat found the little owl's company in the dark oddly comforting.

A steep, slanting climb brought Cat and Tootoo at length to a region of chill air where there were no more branching passages, only the close darkness and a hint of light far ahead.

"Tootoo?"

The little owl was gone. Caution slowed Cat's progress to a snail's creep. As she wriggled the last short distance toward the light, and peered down into the room below, she gasped with pleasure. Sunlight!

Wonder of wonders, it *was*. Shafts of pale, spring sunlight spilled across a dark floor patterned with stars! From her vantage point Cat could see three deep windows and portions of two more. Before the centermost, brooding out over a gold-crested sea of cloud, stood a tall, stooped figure hooded and cloaked in black.

15. THE OWL KING

"See, there. The crystal dome in front of the throne," whispered Fith, making himself as small as possible so that Arl might squeeze in beside him. As soon as the Rokarrhuk guards had locked the Ashkins in their quarters at the work-day's end, Cat, at his urging, had led them to the airwell spy-hole above the Naghar's splendid Pillar Hall.

Arl peered down through the stone screen. "I see. The tray under it . . . how many stones do you think—"

"Twelve." Fith shivered. "There are hollows in the tray for twelve, all the size of your Dreamstone."

"I don't understand. Nine of the Twelve Stones are safe in Thamor. Findral's mother Renga told us so." Arl inched backwards toward the main airwell where Cat crouched, waiting.

"Come," she said. "I'll show you the Naghar's room. It's stranger still."

"Why would an airwell *go* there if the room is as windowed as you say?" asked Fith, always curious.

Cat's answer was a rap on the back of his hand and a finger drawn across his wrist, the sign for silence and sign-speech.

The three companions climbed as cautiously and quietly as snails. From the wide place—a landing of sorts—at the top, Arl slipped down the last short stretch first, and then backed out so that Fith might take a look. The air-well's mouth was hidden among the ceiling's knobbled clumps and clustered spears of dripstone, which blocked a part of the room from their view. The windows that were visible were shuttered against the night, and the room was lit by a hanging lamp. Nine wicks flamed in its nine spouts. There was no sign of the Naghar, or of any guard.

Arl and Fith were as surprised as Cat had been at the homely clutter. There was no reeking crucible or cauldron, no pet Dread One, and the scent in the cool air was of balsam, not the bitter tang of sorcerer's-herb. Heaps of books and papers, dead candles and the remains of forgotten meals covered the long table, shelves, and seats of chairs. The center of the dark stone floor was inlaid in blue with a pointed star, and from the six points visible, four more could be guessed at—a round room, then, with five narrow windows piercing walls that must at their thinnest be five yards thick. Within the O at the star's center, the sign of Lis the Sun was set in gold, and of Mirelidar the Moon in bright vindurn. Evenly spaced around that inner O stood five white wands, fixed upright for sighting stars. The Tiddi recognized their purpose, for Starwise too used wands, sighting along a line between a star-circle wand and some distant landmarker.

Against the wall, beside an alcove of bookshelves, stood a stone perch carved in the shape of a branching tree stump, complete with a sleepy giant of an owl. On a table nearby, a crystal dome—which was the twin of the one in the Pillar Hall—glittered brightly in the lamplight.

As he returned to the darkness of the wider passage, Fith reached for Cat's hand and signed on her palm, "Is the owl alive, or stone?"

"What owl?" Cat whispered, startled. In dismay she

clapped a hand over her mouth, and then slipped back down to see for herself. She returned with dampened spirits to lead the way downward to a hiding hole where they would be safely out of hearing.

"There was no owl before," Cat whispered, "so it cannot be stone. What shall we do? I brought a rope so one of us might slip down to look among the scrolls for a map of the mountain—and to see what the crystal hides. But how can we now?"

"Not with such a guard," Arl agreed. "It is too dangerous. He must be as tall as Fith!"

"With a beak and claws Fith does not care to see any c-closer," said Fith with a shiver. "And I like owls!" He reached up to Tootoo's perch on his shoulder and stroked her breast.

Tootoo, too-too too! The little owl hooted softly in agitation.

Cat scowled. "The longer we are trapped in this ants' nest of a mountain, the more sure it is that Lek will seek and find a way into the same trap. Findral too, if he has come. And they cannot hide in airwells."

She touched her knife where it hung on its cord under the shabby Ashkin tunic. "This Naghar has so many maps, he would not miss one. And the owl sleeps. I could try. I am quick."

"But not so quick as the slowest owl." The softly rasping rebuke came from overhead.

"Hlik!"

Fith spied the raven first. "How did you get in? How did you find us?"

"By the noise you make," snapped Hlik. He was perched on a shallow ledge overhead, where an airwell outlet tilted up to meet the dark sky. He spoke as softly as a night breeze. "And I was in and out of Avel Timrel often in

Basadil's time. Be warned: if there is an owl in the Star Chamber as you say, he knows that you are here, and how many you are. Rest here, and be still. I will take a look at him myself."

The great raven hopped down and, talons clicking softly on the rock, stepped briskly out of sight up the narrow, slanting airway beyond the hiding hole. In a moment he was back and shaking his head.

"That is Hom, chief of the birds of the Owl Mountains, and if he is asleep, I am a stork. It is a great pity, for even one of the scrolls or pages from that table might tell Lek and the Wizard—yes, Ollo came from Aab with Findral— might tell them much about what mischief's afoot here. But Hom knows me, so I dare not show my beak. We are old enemies. We—hold, there!"

Tootoo had suddenly fluttered from Fith's shoulder and Fith, alarmed, lunged after her, but caught only a crack on the head from the low ceiling. Cat, nearest the upward passage, had no better luck. She snatched at the small shadow fluttering past and grasped one small foot, but was left with only a deep scratch for her pains.

They hurried after, and in a moment three Tiddi heads and the raven's ringed the mouth of the downward-tilting Star Chamber airwell. From so far above its opening into the chamber below, they could see little and hear no more, only a faint rustling. Of pages? Parchment leaves?

Silence. And then the sound they feared.

Ho-o-om, hom!

"Quick! Back down to Bort's hiding hole!" Arl commanded, giving Fith a shove.

Fith held back. "But—Tootoo!"

"Tootoo can fly," Hlik said sharply, "but not if her way is blocked by three chattering Tiddi. Go!"

Fith went, with Arl scrambling after and Hlik close behind. Cat, pulling free of her tunic the cord knotted to her knife's sheath, came last—but backwards, facing the way Tootoo must come. She had gone perhaps a furlong when the breathy hiss of an indignant, small bird stopped her. A moment later Tootoo blundered in a wild flutter through the darkness to brush Cat's face with her wings and tangle small talons in her hair. Pulling them free, Cat pressed close against the passage wall and thrust the little owl out behind her to flutter after the others.

Khah! Khah-h-h!

Far above, the faint light from the Star Chamber vent vanished. A breathy hiss of rage, a scrabbling sound, and the rattle of feathers warned that the great owl Hom came in pursuit. That was ill fortune enough but—worse—even if he failed in that pursuit, he would have much to tell his Master. Too much.

Slithering backward, Cat felt as she went for the byway she remembered passing on the right hand on the way up. When her foot touched its emptiness, she wriggled back into the opening and, pulling her knees up under her, waited in a nervous crouch, like a wary peeka watching at its burrow's mouth.

But Cat was a peeka with sharp teeth. As the harsh *Khah-h-h!*, the rustle of the heavy body and the *scritch* of sharp talons drew closer, she slid the ancient Tiddi knife from its sheath. The vindurn blade glowed palely for a moment—a cruel, blue-white sliver of moonlight—before she concealed hand and knife in a fold of her tunic's skirt. Both bait and trap, rapt with a hunter's intentness, she hovered on the edge of motion, scarcely breathing.

The great bird slowed and was silent, listening. If there was any sound from Tootoo and the others, it was too far off for Cat's ears. Why had the owl stopped? She was tempted to stir, to lure him forward, but then he moved again. Cat felt, more than saw, the feathered bulk shouldering closer, the angry, gaping beak . . .

Khah-h-h!

Cat struck.

In the hiding hole, Snip and her uncles huddled together near the entrance as if they half feared Hlik might take it in his mind to fly at them from his perch atop Arl's carrying sack. They knew his name from one of Nabb's scraps out of the Songs but, never having seen such a creature as a raven before, they found his bright, beady eyes, his beak, and his great size as frightening as any of the Naghar's owls.

Fith, knees drawn up to his chest, rocked back and forth in anxious misery. "I should never have brought Tootoo. I should have left her with Qara. Cat told me so. Where *is* Cat?"

Arl was nerving himself to set out in search of her, great owl or no, when there came a soft scratching at the doorstone. Together Arl and Bort rolled it aside and let Cat in.

"What happened?"

"Where have you been?"

"I have been a-killing Hom," Cat said breathlessly. Her arms were streaked with blood, the owl's and her own. "He is in the blind airwell above the Pillar Hall. With stones and mortar to wall him in, the Naghar will never know. He will think Hom went out through the Owlery and never came back. But—look!"

She held out a crumpled square of parchment covered with a spiderwork of lines and fine, small script. "Tootoo *did* snare herself a scrap from the Naghar's table. What is it? Can you tell?"

Hlik cocked an eye at the page over Arl's shoulder and

saw a circular spider's web of crisscrossed lines. Eleven points, pricked onto the web's upper right-hand quadrant, bore names or calculations in a fine, crabbed script.

"Is it a sky chart?" Arl asked.

"*Pr-ruk.* If it is, it is a strange one." Hlik leaned closer. "The circles could be the paths of the Ten Worlds— Tionel, Aturil, Nirim-Earth and the others. When Avel Timrel was Basadil's he used the Star Chamber's wands and windows to chart Mirelidar and the nine sky worlds in their dance. But the loops and crossing lines? No sky world moves so."

"Then it is of no use to us," Cat said impatiently. If only it had been a map! "What of Lek and Findral—and the Wizard? Hlik must tell them to turn back. There is nothing here but danger."

Old Hlik cocked his beady eye at her. "Is danger to be fled, then, Hom's bane?"

Cat's small, pointed chin set stubbornly. "Yes. Better so than offer your neck to be chained. For what? An opal and a name? Besides, in Gzel the Illigan who was Captain there made Lek look in the Naghar's dark Mirror, and Lek bowed his head over the basin of dark water and spoke to it as 'Master.' If he comes here, the Naghar may master him in truth."

"And he'll find no opals bedded in the City's mines or lying in its streams," Fith put in. "Their Singer, Nabb, says the Lord Naghar is greedy for gemstones, but none of any size has been found for many years."

"It is true," Bort said with an uneasy glance at his brothers. "The lazt was a Nemral, and Nabb had the polizhing of it."

"*P-r-ruk!* I shall tell Lek what you say, but I shall take the parchment, too. Perhaps the Wizard can unravel it."

Arl held out the drawing willingly, though he would have liked to puzzle over it awhile. "Good! Tell them the hole we entered by is sealed up, and we must look for the way out by Melurath. Your wizard may know of it."

The great raven nodded. "News or no, I shall come tomorrow eve." So saying, he took up the parchment in his beak and vanished through the vent-hole that led out onto the mountainside.

"Ai, ztars!" Zdil exchanged a look of wonder with his younger brother. "These are ztrange days—the King come, old Hom dead, an then a zcrap of zong that walks an flies an talks! What will be next?"

"King? What King?" asked Fith and Cat together.

But Zdil looked alarmed and then confused and could not be persuaded to explain himself.

In the dark stairwell below the kitchens half an hour later, Fith put his eye to the door's crack to watch the shadows dance.

"They *are* like birds. Long-legged, slow-stepping perrins." Like perrins, both strange and beautiful. But when they came near the curtain wall, suddenly they were very small and Tiddish.

"Why should their Dance so fright the Ashkins, then? And me?" Arl asked. "Because only one Dancer has ever returned from the Dance? All last night I lay weaving my dreams with what we've learned of Avel Timrel, and—"

A faint sound from far above caught his ear, and then the thud of heavy feet on the curving stair.

"We are not safe here," he signed. "Come, this way."

Followed by Bort and Zdil, they slipped out through the door and moved from rubble heap to rubble heap along the stone-curtained gallery encircling the Dancing Floor, stepping quickly as the jangling music rose, hiding when it fell. By the time the footsteps on the stair appeared in the shape of two scowling Rokarrhuk and an

Illigan in a scarlet gown, Arl and Fith were crouched in a dark, shadowed recess in the rock.

Arl shivered, but his eyes gleamed. Almost directly opposite, some fifteen or so feet away, he spied a narrow slit in the stony folds that shrouded the Dancing Floor from their view. But so narrow a breach revealed little. The circular room beyond appeared to be lit by many lamps or torches, for the light that spilled out through the rent in the amber curtain dazzled eyes grown accustomed to darkness and lamp flames hardly larger than a pea.

Fith had a confused impression of brilliant colors flicking past, and once a blank-eyed Tiddi face. Then Arl was tugging at his arm and motioning to the others, and they were off again, moving and staying as the music rose and fell.

Not far from what appeared to be the entrance to the Dancing Floor—an opening screened with heavy leather curtains and guarded by Rokarrhuk—Arl spied the passage of his dream.

"The Wolf's head!" he signed to Fith. "There!"

The archway leading into an outer passage from the gallery where they were hiding was richly carved with vines and fruits and woodland creatures much cracked and worn away with time and rough use. Its keystone was a grinning Wolf's head, an image of one of the ancient Wolves of Aam. A good omen, surely.

"I remember him," Arl signed excitedly. "I thought him one of the Dread Ones and almost cried out as my father carried me under him."

"But—the guards?" Fith's brows made a question of the signs. Torches flared in the outer passage, and in their light the armor of the Rokarrhuk gleamed darkly. They stood rigid, four pairs of goblin statues. Only their eyes moved.

How *had* his mother and father passed the guards? Arl

could not remember. It had been so long ago. Something had happened. Noise and light and—what? Under cover of some great confusion Olf and Oona, with Arl upon his father's back, had raced past a wide, lamplit stairway and down through dark galleries to another stair. But knowing so was no help now.

Arl crept forward along the wall behind a row of tall storage jars. Oil, for the lamps? He craned to see whether the wide corridor beyond the archway was clear. What he saw—the torch brackets shaped like hornflowers, the ancient filigree stone lamps upon the broad stairs stepping down from above—was, gleam for gleam and step for step, as he remembered. Not dreamed, remembered! Entranced, he almost whisked back into the gallery's shadows too late as footsteps came pattering down the stair.

The feet were Nabb's. Bustling, nervous Nabb.

A sullen guard pulled back the curtain, and Nabb scuttled through to the Dancing Floor. Arl and Fith and their companions exchanged a startled look as the music stopped and heavier footsteps sounded on the stairs.

The Illigan Koorg strode through the arch. Behind him marched six Rokarrhuk.

And in their midst, wrists bound, walked Cat.

16. BASADIL'S HAND

FINDRAL PEERED OUT from the crack in the Fennethelen's dark wall where the three searchers had taken shelter for the night, and where Hlik had found them after nightfall. At middlenight, and again at the third and sixth hour after, Rokarrhuk patrols had passed. Hlik had heard the beating of wings and a soft cry that did not reach the others' ears. Great owls, he said. But it was Findral who spied the soldiers astride the giant Dread Ones, as they swept eastward along the river of ice through the blowing snow. Three more hours had passed, but there was no sign yet of their returning.

Still wrapped in cloak and blanket, Lek sat huddled in their narrow shelter and peered, frowning, at the square of parchment Hlik had brought. He shielded it from the falling snowflakes. In the gray dawn it was little more than a blur of lighter gray, but three weeks in the Shadowlands had sharpened his eyes. After a few moments he found that he could make out a faint web of lines.

"I have seen something like this before, but it must have been long ago, for I cannot remember where. The Astronomer Royal had a room full of charts, but . . ." The memory of his days in the Astronomer's House in Kimmer was overshadowed by his unwitting part in the theft of

Nirim the Worldstone. Beside that, all other memories had paled.

Hlik, perched on a rough outcrop above the heads of Men and Wolf, stretched his wings wide and rattled his feathers, shaking himself awake. He craned to see.

"*Pr-r-ruk!* 'Something like'? Like and unlike, I would guess, but then it is an Age since I last saw Basadil at his mapping in the Star Chamber. The eleven points may stand for Lis and the Ten Worlds on their circling paths, but what of the lines that criss and cross?"

"Why, they must be crisscross lines," quipped a sleepy Ollo. He yawned and stretched one leg out, then the other. "What are you talking about?"

"The page Hlik brought from Avel Timrel. The page stolen from the Naghar's chamber," Findral answered hastily before Lek's impatience with the Wizard's lapses into foolishness could prompt a sharp retort.

"Ah, yes. May I see it?"

Suddenly brisk, Ollo thrust his hand out commandingly. Lek responded to the note of authority without thinking, but then scowled. The Wizard slipped in and out of his confusion almost as if it were a cloak he donned and doffed; almost as if he meant to disconcert, to startle the conjuror into—what?

Sitting up, Ollo held the parchment close to his eyes. "Um, hah! If it is a sky map, it was made by a child—or for some purpose not to do with skycasting. Even if the Worlds did spin about Lis all in the same plane, their circles are not so evenly spaced."

"Nor do they reel around Lis all in a row, side by side," observed Findral, looking over the Wizard's arm.

"Um, ah." Ollo's hand dropped, and his eye wandered down the shadowy ravine and out across the dim river of ice. "Do they not?"

Lek grimaced, as if to say "Off again!" and reached to snatch up the stolen chart as it fell from Ollo's hand.

"But they do!" The force of Ollo's exclamation startled even Hlik, who often in the days past had watched, head cocked, as the two Men strove to measure one another. The Wizard clapped his hands together sharply, snatched up his staff, and surged to his feet. His agitation, echoed in a shimmer that crackled like lightning over the billowing folds of his cloak, stiffened raven, wolf, and conjuror in alarm.

"Indeed they do! At the Gathering!" Flourishing his staff to urge the others after him, he strode down out of the narrow ravine. Though there was not yet light enough to see a crevasse a stride away, he sprang up the bank of the ice river and set out eastward at a skimming pace. Once the others had caught up, Hlik settled heavily on Lek's shoulder, the better to hear what news could be so fearful.

"Four times in the last Time, once in this," Ollo said as he strode on, "the Worlds have gathered. Not in so neat a row as on your chart, no—but in the same quarter of Lis's sky. I would guess that its time has come again."

"The Gathering . . ." Findral's eyes glowed, and he danced a little caper in the snow. "I know a Tale that speaks of it. The Wolves of Aam and Tion's folk journeyed here to the Gathering Dance by the Wolf Way."

"Just so." Ollo's bushy eyebrows drew together in a deep frown, and the ridge of his long nose seemed to sharpen. "But now wild Men and slave folk and beasts gather. For what? To guard this Lord Naghar? The Shadowlands do that. To make war upon Astarlind? Upon birds and beasts and a handful of Tiddi? But then the Silvrin would be roused and make a war no outlaw rabble could hope to win, however canny their lord. These patterns—" He crumpled the sheet of parchment in his gloved fist. "Your Tiddi friend's dream of the Shadow Dancers begins to worry me."

"The Dance?" Hlik croaked in horror. "Do you mean that they could counterfeit the Gathering Dance?" He rattled his feathers in agitation, and Lek winced as strong talons dug through cloak and coat to bruise his collarbone.

"At the right hour, with stones from the veins where the Twelve Stones were mined—perhaps." Ollo's cloak billowed out behind him as he lengthened his stride. "In this cursed, clouded land I cannot be sure that it is the Gathering Time. Only astronomers and Silvrin count the old Circle of Years nowadays. If I recall aright, the last Gathering of the Moon and the Ten Worlds was in the reign in Umeár of Dannam, five hundred and some years ago. That was the year the fire mountain buried Ullin in ash, and with it the great Library of Umeár and its loremasters. If it is Gathering Time again, there well may be some great mischief afoot. But what? And why and how? The true Dancing Stones, save Lisar and Nirim, are safe in Thamor—and Mirelidar in Werrick, so you say."

"If there's mischief, there's more deviltry than foolery to it!" With a sharp thrust Hlik lifted into the air, showering snow on Lek and calling as he climbed. "Tinnimoon Eve, the Eve of Spring, falls in three nights. If there is to be trouble, it may come then. Time is short!" Rising in a swift, steep spiral, he vanished into the clouds.

"Where is he off to?" Lek asked. Rubbing his shoulder, he hurried after the Wizard.

"To my folk first," guessed Findral. "And then to find the Silvrin. Some *do* still wander in Astarlind."

"I hope they wander close at hand," Ollo muttered. But then his head lifted and he stopped abruptly, holding up a warning hand. "Listen!"

Faintly through the heavy, shadowed air they heard a high, thin flutter of sound that grew all too swiftly into the strange, blade-sharp whistle of whips they had heard at intervals through the night.

"Rokarrhuk!" Findral wheeled and vanished toward the mountain's cliffs, a white shadow in the falling snow.

"Come!" Lek took the Wizard's elbow and hurried him after the Wolf. "It has not been half an hour since the last patrol. Something *is* afoot. Or else they have found some trace of us this snow's not covered. Hurry, old man! They ride the Dread Ones."

Ollo pulled free. "Come, indeed! You will rush us into a hiding place we'll not climb out of. We are not Wolves, to skim across snow-masked crevasses."

There was a touch of laughter in his tone and, hearing it, Lek turned to look at him in sharp dismay. The dreamy, witless look had returned—and at such a time!

Ollo's fingers upon his wrist held him as fast as any iron fetter.

"Come, Conjuror, only stand quietly, and we shall see them pass us by." As he spoke, hood, gray cloak, and Wizard began to fade, shimmering into whiteness.

"Leave go, old fool! *You* may vanish, but I am no wizard." Craning to see down the snowy westward curve of the valley, he strained to be free. "Leave g—"

Lek found himself held speechless in mid-word and turned to see a faint, snowy shadow of Ollo's bristling frown and chill blue stare.

"Old fool? Impatient *young* fool! It does not matter if you never learned the Transparencies. It can be done. Take a deep breath, still your mind, say *Irsilo nánne silar* twice over, and watch." The Wizard gave his wrist a sharp shake.

Startled, Lek turned away from the sound of the approaching patrol to look down at his imprisoned glove and sleeve and see—and not see—them. For a moment he watched, enthralled, and then in belated obedience withdrew into stillness with the words and watched the spell wrap itself about him. Dimly he saw Findral's white shadow come questing back across the snowy ice to find them by their footprints. No other trace was left but these, and an airy gap where no snow fell.

"Wonderful!" said Findral with a white grin. But for the gray shadows that poured toward them along the ice, he could have stood and marveled until Ollo wearied and the spell faltered. Instead, seeing that they stood only a little aside from the way that the sweeping line of Dread Ones and their Rokarrhuk riders must pass, he stretched his length across both pairs of unseen boots to hide their telltale prints. The falling snow and the uncanny magic of the Wolves of Aam made him so convincing a drift of snow that except for the weight upon his feet even Lek, standing above him, would not have known he was there.

"Excellent beast!" murmured Ollo.

A moment later Dread Ones, running six abreast, were upon them and past, with a high, shivering cry that sprang from one Rokarrhuk to the next. The nearest of the giant wolves veered and almost stumbled as he passed, but recovered quickly at the slash of his rider's whip and sped on.

Lek shuddered and let out a long sigh of relief. "And I had hoped never to see such creatures again! I felt the nearest's breath upon my face. I could have put out my hand and touched its flank."

"As well you did not," Ollo observed drily. He shook out the folds of his reappearing cloak. "The goblin's whip would have caught you and, as interesting as it might be to know whether an invisible arm bleeds transparent blood, I am glad not to have learned the answer just yet."

"The Dread One nearest Lek scented us. I am sure of it," Findral said. "That one will not pass us by again for any magic!"

Lek brushed snow from his hood and shoulders. "Ai! If our hurrying needed another spur, that would do excellently. How far now to your Sun's Gate, Master Ollo? If the stars decree disaster for Tinnimoon Eve, there's precious little time to snatch our Tiddi friends safely away."

Conjuror and Wizard matched long strides for several moments in silence before Ollo stirred himself to answer. "Twenty leagues, perhaps. But if I fear aright, it will not be the stars, but your Naghar who decrees."

"I see no door." Lek stood with his back to the east wind, his cloak tightly wrapped around him, and spoke to Ollo in weary disbelief. "Four times in twenty leagues you have spied this 'door,' and four times it has proved to be no portal, but a shadow, or lichen, or a stain upon the rock. It is near two days since Hlik came out of Nagharot. Who knows what danger the little folk may have fallen into?"

"There's time enough, time enough," the Wizard answered testily. "If it is not here it cannot be far off, and we have two days until Tinnimoon Eve." But under the brim of his hood he wore a worried look.

"'Time enough'! 'Safe enough'! Only if our Tiddi friends keep to the hiding hole Hlik told us of, and that is as likely as snow in Sarimoon."

Findral the Wolf frowned as he too watched Ollo run his hands lightly over the sheer black rock, now and again brushing away a film of crusted snow. Last Sarimoon there *had* been snow in Astarlind. On Midsummer morning.

"Where were you on Midsummer last?" he asked Lek.

Something in the young Wolf's voice made Lek turn with a quizzical look. "Do you mean there *was* snow? On Midsummer day I was—five days out from Umeár in a roaring sea. It was a storm that blew out of nowhere."

"Pah!" Master Ollo moved along the cliff face. "Nothing comes out of nowhere. Not even wizards can give nothing a shape. We must have at least thin air to work with. And we can waken things that sleep."

With a sweep of his hand he brushed away a thin crust of snow from the rock, and where his hand had passed the snowy imprint of another hand stood out against the cliff's dark face: a hand raised palm-up, as if in greeting.

"Great Lis! Is it Basadil's Hand?" cried Findral.

Lek drew back a little. "Basadil's Hand? Then it *is* the Sun's Gate. But if entrance must be won by Basadil's Hand—from what I read of it long ago in old Azra's books —it is no good to us. We cannot pass. Unless you, Wizard, are more than you seem."

"Or you, my young friend." Ollo looked at him consideringly. "And I must say, it seems very careless of your Master Azra not to lock up his books. No telling what mischief a youngster might put his hand to with a wizard's library. You are right about Sun's Gate, though. It will not open for the asking, however potent the spell."

He brushed the snow from the shallow imprint and, pulling off his right glove, laid his hand against the mountain's, palm to palm.

Nothing. Sky and mountain loomed as darkly over the day's stillness as before.

Ollo sighed. "There, I knew it! Beware all tales of half-elvish great-great-grandmothers. I have as much Silvrin blood as friend Findral here. Come, Kell of Umeár. Try your hand."

"Mine? Your wits are still addled, old man! All this time we've looked for a door you could not open? We have wasted more than a day. If this road is not for us, we must turn back. We must reach the tunnel the Rokarrhuk guard and try if your vanishing trick will take us past them. Forty leagues! It will mean no sleep, and little rest."

Ollo's blue gaze looked no less vague than before, but his voice was as cold and hard as iron. *"Kell!* Try your hand, I say."

Lek flinched at the sound of his old name, as if pride or some old wound had been touched upon the quick. He stiffened, but held back the sharp answer that sprang to his tongue. Stripping off his glove, he thrust out the right hand he always took pains to conceal. "Much good it will do. I am left-handy. But you know that."

Ollo shrugged. "So are many."

"Not in Umeár."

"No? But then we are not in Umeár," the Wizard answered gravely.

Impatient with such woolly foolishness, Lek unclenched his hand, the hand that was so strangely small: strongly shaped, though faintly crooked and scarred upon the palm. Measured against the handprint in the rock, the curved fingers might have been a boy's.

But as his palm pressed against the stony one, the great leaves of the Sun's Gate swung open.

17. DANCE!

IT WAS LIKE FLYING, Cat had thought. Not floating. Flying, though her guards stumped heavily along beside her: down a stair, along a footway skirting a dark well, past crystal-flowered pools. A curving stair. A path, another stair. Cat's feet had touched each tread as lightly as a moth's foot, and at each touch she flew, wingless, on her downward way. The heavy boots of the four Rokarrhuk soldiers struck sparks from each stone step, but the sound they made was *Tling-tling-tling*, like crystals strung upon a silver wire to tinkle in the wind. It was very strange . . . and the crystals that hung on the silken fringe of Koorg the Illigan's belt clashed and clanged together like iron hammers beating on the City's walls.

The potion. Her confusion had begun with the potion she was forced to drink once her arms were safely pinioned. She had kicked, but only bruised her feet against the soldiers' rock-hard shins. *"A knive—zhe has a wicked knive."* A terrified Ashkin squeak. Nabb. Nabb, looking fearful and excited and despairing, all at once.

Nabb, returning late to the Ashkins' quarters, had reported seeing a tiny owl attacked by two larger ones near the Owlery, and Cat—fearing for Tootoo, whom she had supposed to be with Fith—had darted for the airwell. The Rokarrhuk guards were waiting in the Owlery's dark shadows: leathery hands and biting cords, and the bitter drink.

Nabb, still squeaking and wringing his long fingers, scuttled off to the right along the passage at the stair's foot—a small, elderly rat, a foolish reed-rat grown hopeful of the marsh-cat's mercy. How many Ashkin secrets, how many darkle children had he betrayed, Nabb with his twitching rat's tail? No . . . that was not right. Nabb had no tail. It was the Illigan, gliding before her, who had a tail. A long, furred cat's tail that with each step lashed gently below the stiff gown's hem.

As the little procession passed from the lamplit passage crossing through the shadows of the gallery that encircled the Dancing Floor, Cat's gaze wandered over the glowing rose and golden draperies of stone and marveled at seeing them seem to stir and gently billow to the music. The brilliant light that spilled from the room within hurt her eyes, and she turned her face toward the shadows.

Cat's darksight was not so sharp as Fith's or Arl's. But now, as she stood in her daze, waiting while a doorguard took a message from the Illigan into the Dance, she found that she could see into the dark heart of the deepest shadow. And there—there in the shadows were Arl and Fith and Bort and Zdil crouched down behind a straggling row of storage jars!

Cat smiled her delight. She lifted her bound hands to sign *Why are you hiding?* and found she could not. Opening her mouth to call out, she saw alarm widen Arl's eyes. His whitened face and arms and feet, his round, startled eyes made him seem a comic painting of himself. A painting on a wall . . . Bort, beside him, leaned close to whisper in his ear, and Arl began frantically to sign over and over again the alarm *Silence! Danger! Silence!*

Obediently, Cat's gaze grew blank and wandered back

to the Rokarrhuk and the bright doorway, Arl and Fith and the Ashkins promptly forgotten. Then, abruptly, the smiling spell that bound her wavered, and she half wakened into fear. A second Illigan, taller, green-gowned, came gliding through the drooping Dancers, a figure both terrifying and familiar.

And this time it really was the Captain of Gzel.

But you . . .

Her mind shaped the words her lips could not, and in answer the Illigan's short upper lip stretched itself into an unaccustomed smile. His round yellow eyes glowed. With a mocking bow, he addressed her in the Old Speech.

"But I am dead? No, little princess, we meet again. You are surprised! And disappointed, I fear. You thought our brief meeting in Gzel the end of me? Oh, your giant friend's knife was sharp, but an Illigan's heart rides higher than a Man's. I called. My servants found me. And since the wise captain has forethought for his own skin, at the mountain's first rumble we were lowered to the Ice in the cask that brought snow up to melt for water."

The Captain of Gzel laughed softly. Turning, he gave a sharp order to one of the Rokarrhuk in a strange, harsh tongue. It sent the guard at a hasty trot along the gallery past the dusty storage jars to the shadowy stair down which Arl and his companions had come. When he had gone, the Man-beast reached out and drew Cat after him through the leather curtains onto the Dancing Floor. The guards, their duty overcome by curiosity, crowded close to the curtains' opening to watch. At the center of the Floor the Illigan loosed Cat's arm, but held her fast with his hard, yellow gaze.

"The Lord Naghar will have many questions for you, small one: how you came here, and who and where your companions are. Tiddi!" He shook his round head wonderingly. "All this long age the Naghar has fortified this land with darkness that turns away the wise elf or Iceling and peopled it with shadowed hearts—yet in walk these little mouseling folk as blithe as if they came to picnic in a mushroom cave."

Cat, numbed both by fear and the strange drink that had been forced upon her, stood rooted, speechless, and could only raise her bound hands to her breast in a gesture of protest. Yet even as she did so, her sleepy wits stirred. At the pressure of her wrist, a small, cheering glow of warmth grew against her breastbone. Lek's shard of stone! It had hung forgotten on its cord beneath her tunic, and Cat felt a small glow of defiance awaken with it.

"I—I do not unnerztan." Cat struggled to free the words. "I am Dolo, Z-Zard's daughter."

"Ah. Indeed. And why should Zard's daughter have been prowling in the Upper City?"

"I wentoo the Owlery—to z-zteal eggs." Cat cringed away from him and closed her eyes as if against the glare and dazzle of the sheaves of torches that stood in iron standards around the wide floor. "Please. I am avraid. I am lame. I cannot danze!"

But there was no escaping so easily. Cat saw the Illigan's yellow gaze even behind her eyelids and knew he listened at her thoughts even as she struggled to command them. Slowly, unwillingly, her head dragged up. Her eyes opened.

The Illigan's eyes glittered. "Not dance? I said in Gzel that you had come at need. And so you have again. You think some foolish errand drew you here? No. It was the Lord Naghar's need that brought you. His will. The mountain-maggots' dances are the broken echoes of an echo, but your folk . . . Oh, you will dance!"

Unsheathing the knife at his belt, he cut the cord that bound her wrists. Then he made a sign to two dull-eyed

Ashkins crouching by the wall. These two lifted wooden tubes to their lips and set the strange, sliding music to wailing softly. As it swelled slowly to fill the heavy air, the Illigan opened the small pouch hanging beside his knife's sheath and, taking from it a pinch of blue powder, held it before Cat's face and puffed it into her eyes. The torchlight vanished, and with it the musicians, the drooping Dancers, chamber, the Illigan and gaping guards—and Arl, seizing his chance, flitting silently under the Wolf's-head arch and down the long lamplit passage—all.

Rubbing her eyes, Cat looked around her in slow amazement. Surely . . .

She stood in the Song Circle on the hill's crest above Eem at first light. Had she dreamed it all—Everdark, the Ashkins, Hom of the sharp beak? No matter. Lis waited, and if the rest slept, then Cat must dance her up! Crossing her hands upon her breast, she hummed the old tune of *Lisárelo glanagal meir* and slowly folded downward until she sat crosslegged and, bowing, touched her forehead to Nirim, the earth. Unfolding into the Dance, she mimed the Sun's slow leap into the sky, and then the patterns of the Dance became more formal, more complex: not the simple round suggested by its old name of "Lisar's Circle," but an intricate, shifting, interlacing spiral.

Scarcely had she finished when—most strange—Lis hung in the west, her foot upon Nummas, the tallest peak of the Blue Mountains. Strange indeed, but Cat set obediently to dancing her safely down to sleep, moving with a hunter's lithesome grace, half cat, half willow. Sundown, moonrise, moonfall. Each followed hard upon the other, and her flying feet wove their patterns on the dream-earth. Leafspring, Midsummer, Leaffall, Midwinter, Loorimoon, Trillimoon, moon after moon . . .

Now: the Gathering.

Gathering?

Dance it. The Gathering.

Cat looked around her uncertainly. Gathering—what? Wineberries? Grapes? Wrinklenuts?

Eem's Song Circle faded. She stood, alone and bewildered, in the dusk between dream and waking. How long she wandered there, she did not know, but when she woke, footsore and weary, she stood not on the Dancing Floor, but before the empty throne in the darkened Hall of Pillars in the upper region of the City.

Alone.

A few lamps burned, small crystal globes hung from the starry roof, but in so huge a space their light was faint. The glow that shimmered dimly on the towering columns and winked among the ceiling's stars came from the crystal-domed bowl on its slender crystal pedestal in the center of the room. The dome shone like a fat silver moon in a night-blue sky.

All this Cat saw clearly, but not caring, as if she walked apart from herself, or in a dream. On the dais, facing the crystal moon, stood the massive throne of black glass, with a tasseled cushion of green silk. Yet for all her weariness, it was not the cushioned seat that drew Cat, but a dark column to the left of the far, shuttered windows. Of an even blacker glass than the throne, it mirrored her shadowy, approaching self, and she drew close, entranced. Here was no rippled reflection in the River Minning, no scrap of eye and brow in a cup of water!

She had never seen herself as others saw her, until now. Taller than Harr, than Horsey, than any Tiddi, the figure in the column was as thin as a willow withy, with curly hair that would seem almost straight beside a Tiddi's. The toes and fingers were sadly short. *Ugly.* No wonder Old Nar sometimes growled at her, or that softhearted Nar, his son—who nursed crippled birds and once kept a lame piggar for a pet—befriended her. Her ears were pointed, well-shaped Tiddi ears and her face a heart-shaped Tiddi face, but the eyes . . . Shadowed and dark-lashed, at first they too seemed dark, for the light was at her back and the strange Cat in the column all in shadow, but as she came closer still she saw in dismay and dawning wonder how light they were. And leaf-shaped. Like . . .

Cat leaned closer still, but as her fingers brushed the glass she felt the touch of other eyes and then, with the cool, polished stone against her palms, saw them: cold, pale eyes, deep in the pillar's heart.

Stay, granddaughter. I shall come for you.

Cat whirled. The voice had come from—where? The air? The dark pillar's glassy deeps? Her own mind? Suddenly she was frighteningly awake. Her hand felt for the reassuring warmth of Lek's stone beneath her tunic as she looked anxiously along the shadowed ranks of pillars. No one. Nothing.

A moment later, only yards away, a thread of light cleft the starry wall between two columns and widened to reveal a tall, narrow door. A brief flicker of lamplight showed a spiral stair beyond, and then the doorway was filled with shadow. The Naghar stood before her, cloaked and hooded as she had glimpsed him in the Star Chamber.

Tall and a little stooped, his face in shadow, the Lord of Nagharot stood and stared as if Cat were the serpent and he the spellbound ticka bird.

"Arda!" he whispered at last. "You are her image. The Illigans could not know. They could not know!"

Seeing Cat's bewilderment, he laughed, loudly, and threw back his hood. He was white-haired and hawk-faced. His laughter was harsh and rusty, as if it had been long unused.

"The stars in their courses are mad indeed! I set a babe afloat in an ocean storm because she had the clear eyes and the left hand that once defied me—and threatens still in dreams. Yet here she is, by some marvel cast upon the shore of the Old World's last evening, to serve me!"

Cat let her hand fall slowly. The touch of the hidden stone had grown warm against her breast, and suddenly she was certain of what the Tiddi had guessed in Aye on the night of the flood. It *was* a bit of the Tinnelstone, the Wolf Star's Stone! If she had betrayed the old Dances after being forced to drink the Rokarrhuks' potion, at least she would not betray what was left of Tion's Stone.

In his excitement the Naghar paced up and down upon the patterned floor. "In two thousand years the Sky has not smiled on me as she will do tonight—Springday Eve and Tinnimoon Eve and Gathering! Such a thing has never happened in all the years I have sought the pattern of the Great Dance. What does it matter that you know no Gathering Dance? What can it be but the sum of *all* the dances? Now—now the Worlds will dance to my will!"

His dark eyes blazed as he stepped down into the shallow well before the throne and strode to the crystal moon upon its pedestal.

"For I shall fashion the Great Dance anew with the last true daughter of Tion's race—and this!"

At the touch of his hand, the dome opened.

And Lisar, the Sunstone lost since the Times Before, blazed out.

18. THE WIZARDS' WAY

THE SUN'S GATE, the road under the Fennethelen, climbed, all the first day, beside the channel of the Rush, a stream once deep and wide but in these latter days spilling down its ancient path with more froth than force. For caution's sake, Ollo led the way in darkness, striking a light with the tip of his staff only after their way parted from the road. At the parting of the ways, the Sungate Road led up over the hurrying Rush in two broad flights of stairs. It went, Ollo said, steeply and straightly on its way to the Inner Gate that opened out onto the circling valley Basadil's folk called Annul. The Rush came down by a lower path, passing under Annul Vale from Avel Timrel itself.

"And how does he know, I wonder?" murmured Lek to Findral as he stepped down into the water to follow the wizard into the stream's dark mouth.

"From books!" called Ollo briskly, as if the soft question had been meant to reach him over the water's rush. "In the Times Before it was known as the 'Wizards' Way.'"

Findral grinned as he splashed along at the Wizard's heels. "Because it is a climb better suited than the other to old shanks?"

"Impertinent beast! No. In those days these waters that wet your young shins were so fierce that only by wizardry could a traveler pass this Rushmouth. Few knew its secret. As a boy I was taught all the gates and paths and halls of Avel Timrel by my own Master, the Silvrin Tillon. One day, he said, I would be glad of the knowledge."

Once having passed under the road, the tunnel of the Rush opened out into a series of small, climbing caverns. Though night had fallen in the outer world, time was short, so they did not stop to rest or sleep. Only at midmorning—as they guessed it—did Ollo dim his light to a firefly glow and slow his pace.

"Listen!"

T-t-ttt-tap tip-t-t-t-tap.

Faintly, a dull, blurred tapping sounded in the rock. In the half hour following, though still dim and far off, the tapping grew by degrees louder and more distinct. Then, as the course of the Rush bent upward to the right, the sound faded and was left behind, drowned by the falling stream.

"Miners," Ollo said. "If all of their workings lie to the south they will not have discovered this passage.

"But—Tchah! Miners in the old mines! We fear aright, I think. If this Naghar means to bend the Gathering Dance to some dark game, then he must find and shape likenesses of the Twelve Stones. He will have done as you meant to do in replacing the lost Stone Nirim, Conjuror. He will have sought their doubles in the same depths where the Twelve were found. A perfect stone might have at least a shadow of the virtue of its exemplar even though it has not known the mystery of Kyth's reshaping hand. It is no wonder the little folk akin to the Tiddi are held here by your Naghar. The Tiddi of old were masters of Kyth's art.

The splendors of Avel Timrel owe much to the Tiddi gemseekers and stoneshapers."

"I do not see the purpose," said Findral.

"Nor I," Lek said. "I sought only Nirim's appearance, not its power. On Umeár it was known only as a treasure, a ceremonial 'thing.'"

Ollo made a sound more snort than laugh. "This Naghar, whether he is a bandit, wizard, or king, does not sound like one to be content with appearances. We do not see the purpose because we do not know the Purposer."

Findral considered. "The Shadowlands are not mentioned in the Wolf Tales until the Tales of Frear's time, long after the Coming of the Ice. Even so, that was still a hundred hundred years ago. If the Shadow is this Naghar's work—"

Lek stopped, amazed. "A thousand years? What sort of creature *is* he, then? Even in the Times Before, few mortals lived to such an age."

"A sorcerer, then?" said Findral, his eyes gleaming. "Or some Silvrin prince like Arrn of old, who joined with Men to war on his own kind?"

Ollo slowed his pace, then he stopped too. He tapped his nose thoughtfully. "Perhaps. But sorcerers, my bushytailed friend, are for the most part mere Men too, like wizards; and there are still wizards who dwelt among the Silvrin in the Times Before and remember the Wolf-King Frear. Their magic can hold time at bay, though it cannot conquer it. The oldest Circle of Wizards is much dwindled. Of the fourteen, five are dead: Gaetan of old age, Tremme and Visti in the Wars of Aam, and Giurlan in a storm at sea. Seven are left beside Orrin and myself. The seven are all easily accounted for, as are the members of the two lesser Circles. But sorcerers are another matter. They keep to themselves. Power-hungry princes or embittered scholars, they learn their arts in secret and guard their powers jealously. For all I know, there might be three or thirty in the world. And this Naghar may well be of their number."

With a frown the Wizard turned and strode on in silence, until they came to a cavern where the water's noise was all around them.

"Ah, here is the Water Stair!" Ollo said. "We are inside Avel Timrel itself."

The cavern at its far end narrowed to a rough, natural stair, down which the Rush fell in a narrow, heavy ribbon from an opening near the roof. At its side the Wizards' Way climbed the seven broad, steep steps to the stair's head.

"*Taliretir enzili,*" said Ollo, thrusting his staff into the water as he spoke. For a moment nothing happened, and then the flow abruptly ceased. With a nimbleness surprising for one of his years, the Wizard sprang up into the dripping channel and strode on. At its upper end the waterway broadened into a second climbing stair, low-roofed enough to make both Lek and the Wizard stoop. Gaining its top step, Ollo raised his staff to write upon the air and release the waters. Instead, he made a sudden, warning gesture.

At the far side of the dimly lit room above the water stair, a small white figure stood. Sopping wet, half-crouched, it peered upward into a dark, round, dripping hole above its head. A small window half-closed by rubble provided light enough for the three spellbound travelers to see within the overhead hole a stout, iron staple wide enough to be a ladder rung. Clearly the shaft must until moments before have carried the stream down from the City above. The Rush might be no match for its ancient self, but to brave the shaft while the water ran unbound still would take a desperate heart.

Lek and Ollo hesitated, but Findral's nose was sharper than their eyes. In the same moment that Ollo once more lifted his staff to the waters, the great Wolf bounded up the last step and across the sandy floor.

"Arl!"

19. YOUNGLES' GAMES

It was beyond Fith's understanding. The Naghar had called Cat "granddaughter." Granddaughter! Surely she was a Tiddi, however tall, however pale in winter.

Kneeling at the airwell opening high above the Pillar Room's patterned floor, Fith strained to see the Naghar's face but could make out no feature in its hooded shadow. He watched helplessly as Cat was taken by the wrist and drawn toward the stair leading to the Star Chamber high above. Fists clenched, heart a-thump, he almost cried aloud, *"Fight! Wake up and fight! You mustn't dance. You mustn't! Wake and fight!"* Cat's spellbound air as she drifted after her captor and out of sight frightened him, and he whimpered softly. *Cat!*

Yet all might not be lost. If Bort's game worked, there might be a chance of escape for all of them. And it would work, if only the Naghar stayed awhile in his Star Chamber. The signal was Fith's to give.

He took Tootoo onto his hand. "Remember," he whispered in the Old Speech, "say to the Illigan, 'Enemies! North of the Fennethelen!' The creature in the blue gown. Find him and say it."

"Emmies," piped Tootoo with an owlish look of surprise at hearing herself. "Nort."

It would have to do. "Quickly!" Fith whispered. He

dropped the little owl down through the starry stone sky
and saw her disappear through the door into the anteroom.

Minutes later, Fith wriggled down to the opening near
the ceiling of the storeroom corridor. Bort and Zdil and a
strange Ashkin crouched there waiting.

"Zzzt!" Zdil hissed. "Urry. Nabb comes, Gelly zays. By
the near ztair, an Koorg not var behind."

Peering down over his shoulder, Fith saw half a dozen
others lurking in the shadows of the stoneworkers' storeroom opposite.

Bort trembled, suddenly dismayed. "What if Arl's
dreams lie? What if ee has not vound Melurath? Youngles'
games played with words may not work with deeds."

"Too late now," whispered Zdil. "Here comes Nabb . . .
Here he . . . *hup!*"

They jumped.

Nabb, passing below, did not manage so much as a
squeak. Four youngles leaped upon him, clapped long fingers over his mouth, and dragged him hurriedly into the
dark storeroom while six more danced around excitedly.
Then, while Nabb was being bound and gagged, Bort and
three of the others swarmed back up the rippled wall to
the ledge that masked the airwell. Fith, kneeling in the
storeroom shadows, fished his dart pipe from the pouch he
carried under his Ashkin jerkin. He fitted to it a sleep dart
and laid another ready beside his knee.

As the sound of striding, booted footsteps rang along the
passage, more youngles than one shivered and wished to
hear them hesitate and turn back toward the stair. But
though the Illigan Koorg, taller than a Man and striding
with a beast's easy grace, was a vastly more alarming prey
than Nabb, his very arrogance betrayed him. It was un-
thinkable that nine spindly mountain children should leap
from nowhere upon his back and shoulders. He was

Koorg! By the time he realized that it had truly happened, it was too late. A bag that had carried stone dust (and still held a good measure of it) was pulled over his head and tied, and twenty more small figures scuttled out from the dark storeroom to swarm atop him.

Panting, Tiddi hung on the Illigan's arms and lashing tail and dragged at the skirts of his gown, while others flung themselves upon him, bearing him down at last in a tangle of arms and legs. Like a swarm of ants bearing away an overturned beetle, they dragged Koorg into the storeroom, and Fith and Bort pushed the door shut only moments before four Rokarrhuk guards came stumping past at the head of a party of stoneworkers.

Fith peered out, while behind the tall stacks of cut stones the puffing, scuffling sounds of struggle died away. "Won't the soldiers miss Koorg?"

Bort shook his head. "They will think him on zum errand vor the Naghar. Ee was zpying on his zpy, I think." He felt for the lamp niche beside the door. One sharp, scratching *snick!* struck a spark to the oily lampwick.

Two lumpy parcels wrapped in swaths of sacking and much-knotted nettings of rope—one Tiddi-size and one the size of an Illigan—stood upright in a small alcove already half walled up and fitted with a generous airhole by busy young stonefitters.

"When the wall is vinished, two or three muzt ztay to zhift a ztack of ztones in front of it," Bort said. He explained with a sigh, "We cannot hurt old Nabb. Zneak an zpy ee may be, but, you zee—ee does tell a good tale, an we would mizz that. We will just leave im to worry awhile."

Fith put his ear to the door's crack. "All's quiet. Now, where is the Owlery from here?" He eased the door open.

Bort took up a tool sack and led the way.

.   .   .

Fith ruffled Tootoo's breast feathers. "You are the most excellent of owls, little messenger! When we passed the barracks airwell, the Rokarrhuk were lacing up their armor. They were all a-buzz and sounded fierce. 'Enemies —yah! North of the Fennethelen? Hah!' "

Bort, working at the lock on the Owlery door with a graving tool, grinned as he heard it click fast. To fill the keyhole with quick-drying stone mortar was only a moment's work.

"There! If all the Karrugs vrom the barracks trot out an away, we've only two or three zcore left to ztop uz." Bort drew a deep breath. "Unlezz the Naghar zmells trouble an orders the Dread Ones in before the gate is jammed."

The very name of the giant wolves gave Fith a sinking feeling. He had felt their breath and seen their teeth half a year ago, and dreamed of them still. Now, pattering behind Bort across the passage to the airwell they had come by, he felt far more frightened than he had in the raid on the fortress of Gzel. Here there were no formidable allies—no Icelings or Wolves of Aam! What good was a plan to lure guards away from the Dancing Floor, when they had the Illigan who was Captain in Gzel to command them? One Illigan could make up for the slow wits of an army of Rokarrhuk—and the Captain was to be doubly feared for the hatred he must bear the Tiddi who had helped to destroy his citadel. Arl had trembled so at the sight of him that it was a wonder to Fith that he could, as soon as the guards' backs were turned, dart so swiftly through the arch and off to find the half-remembered way to Melurath.

"Don't forget the Illigan of Gzel," Fith warned Bort grimly as he clambered over the airwell's ledge behind him.

"Or Vordibee," chimed in a whisper from the darkness ahead.

"Vordibee? What of him?" Bort's voice was anxious.

"Trouble. Ee's found out. About Nabb an Koorg," Gelly whispered. "Ee zays we muzt ztop, or ee will warn the Naghar imzelf. You muzt come at once. Ee commands it."

"Youngles!"

Vordibee the Wise made a sign for several of the mountain folk to stand by the guards' listening hole beside the door and whisper about harmless things, then he turned to look despairingly from Bort to Gelly to Fith. He seemed to be frightened, angry, and—what? To Fith he had the dithering look of an aged mousel far from home and safety, who sees the snow fox snuffling at his tracks. *Where to go? What to do?*

The old Ashkin wrung his long fingers nervously, then tapped a shaky tattoo on the arm of his chair. "Not be mizzed? Koorg? Of courze ee will be mizzed. *Is* mizzed! Karrugs will be zcouring every hall an ztoreroom. We will all of uz be punished for your foolhardinezz. It muzt ztop. Now! Where are Zdil an Dazz an the others?"

Bort hung his head and mumbled. "In the airwells, watching at the pazzage crozzings."

The crowded chamber was silent, and the wide-eyed pale faces looked to Fith half fearful and half fiercely longing.

"At the crozzings?" Vordibee moaned. "They will be found! Oh, foolish youngles! Hom is dead, but Hom's volk are not. If it is learned you use the airwells, the Naghar will call in all the owl volk an zet them to burrowing."

"He can call, but they will not come." Fith, not so in awe of the old Ashkin as Snip's uncles, spoke up loudly. "I m-mean, they cannot come beyond the Owlery."

Vordibee's agitation deepened. "You have ztopped them? How?"

"Stone paste," Fith said.

"Ztone pazte?" Vordibee's astonished snort was echoed here and there around the room, but many ears pricked up in excitement.

"Nabb's special kind," Fith said. "We painted it on all the roosts in the Owlery, and then Bort locked the door and hatches to the corridor and filled the locks with quick mortar. When the owls come flying in and find they can go no further, they will settle down to roost—and stick fast."

Startled out of his gloom, old Vordibee laughed and slapped his chair's arm, but just as quickly sank back and recovered his frown. "It is as bad as the other! And there is no undoing it." He looked accusingly at Fith. "Wisdom would have given you an your friends to Koorg on the first day. What *elze* have you done?"

Fith drew a deep breath. "The N-north Gate. It may by now be shut against the Dread Ones and Rokarrhuk in the valley camp—and the night-watch soldiers from the upper barracks hall. They had—er, a warning of enemies north of the Fennethelen."

Vordibee held up a hand to still the murmur that ran across the chamber. At his nod, Fith went on to tell in a rush of words of the parchment from the Star Chamber, of all that he had seen and heard in the Hall of Pillars—Cat's peril and the mysterious danger threatened by the Dance —and of Arl's search for the waterfall he had seen in a dream of Melurath.

"*Melurath?*"

Melurath! The Ashkins stirred uneasily, but Fith saw, here and there in the sea of watchful, anxious eyes, gleams too bright for fear.

Vordibee snorted. "Melurath again! An after you have znatched your friend from the Dance you will flee the Mountain. An we will pay the price. Lobbers!"

"No!" burst out young Gelly. "The ideas were more ours than Fith's. Ours an our fathers' an our granfathers'."

Proudly Gelly told how Bort had made a patchwork plan out of youngle games and make-believe, old and new: of Jumpem, with its laughing grownups borne to the floor by the sheer weight of small youngles; of Hauntem, in which they taunted and lured Rokarrhuk astray with ghostly voices; of Trackem, long hours of scuttling through the airwells, following guards on their rounds from barracks to hall to storeroom. Every watchpost was known; every barracks room. When Bort asked for how many minutes the North Gate guardroom stood empty during the changing of the guard, Dazz had known the answer.

"*An* how many zacks of ztone an mortar to vreeze the great wheel that opens the Gate," he finished triumphantly.

Vordibee, despite himself, began to look less stern. In his almost forgotten childhood he had played the same airwell games—until the bitterness of his people's long captivity made such games seem a sad counterfeit of freedom.

"And how many would it take?"

"Only zix." Gelly grinned.

"Zix. An zix of you are mizzing. 'Watching at the crozzways'? Or off meddling with the gatewheel?" Old Vordibee shifted nervously in his seat, but his fingers had stopped their tapping and under his frown his pale eyes were thoughtful.

"What of the hundred Karrugs ztill in Everdark? What of them?"

"We meant to trick them down into the mines," Bort said nervously, "and zhut them up there. Fith has the key."

Fith held out Koorg's keys on their ring. Vordibee took and jingled them as Bort explained. Many Rokarrhuk, he said, had been whipped for pocketing small beryls and chrysopras from the workings, for they coveted gems as greedily as their Master. If two or three Rokarrhuk were to overhear whispers that Koorg had left the shaft hatch unlocked at the workshift's end and was now gone out of Everdark, the temptation must surely be too much for them. Along the passage north of the shaft mouth were storerooms full of stony rubble waiting to be tumbled down after them. Digging out would take the Karrugs days, and still they would have the heavy hatch to deal with.

"Then we zet the Danzers free, an all zlip out by Melurath into the World Beyond."

"Poh!" said Vordibee. "It would take a week to znare the Karrugs in zuch a way, for each would keep the rumor to himzelf. Time is too zhort." He sank back wearily. "To the World Beyond, indeed! If we end up in the lockpits we zhall be fortunate. Come, where are Nabb and Koorg? What are we to do with them? Call the Karrugs? Zend olders to free them?"

"If you will not help," Fith said proudly, "s-surely you can wait for Arl. Let us try to free Cat and the Sunstone ourselves. Arl will think of something!"

"Arl? Ah."

The uncomfortable exchange of looks between old Vordibee and the olders on their benches puzzled Fith. He turned to Snip's uncles, but their pale faces grew pink and they looked down at their feet.

"If young Arl has vound Melurath, ee will not be back," Vordibee the Wise said bitterly. "Ee is Olf's and Oona's youngle, an they left us here in our old darkness. Ee will too."

Even as he spoke, heads turned at the slow creak of the chamber's heavy door. Round eyes grew rounder in wonder as it opened.

The six Rokarrhuk guards who had been posted at the door were stretched on the corridor floor in sleep and Arl, dart pipe in hand, stood in the doorway's arch with one arm across the shoulders of a large gray wolf.

"A wizard, and a conjuror too?" Old Vordibee was dazed. "It is too much for me."

"They have gone looking for the Star Chamber and left your guards to us," Arl said. "What has happened? Why are you all still here?"

A clear way parted for Arl across the crowded chamber as he caught sight of Fith and moved to join him. As frightened as the Ashkins were of Findral, they quickly closed in behind, pressing near to touch and hear.

"They are here because I thought to ztop this mizchief, but it is gone beyond ztopping," Vordibee said heavily. "I no longer know what is right to do. You come with bright eyes an knives an zongs—an now wolves an magicians—an zay, 'Believe uz!' An zo you zteal our youngles' hearts like Lobb zo long ago."

The old Ashkin stood, a tiny figure of great dignity, and bowed.

"Very well," he said. "We will follow as you lead, Oona's son. For you are Haag's only grandzon, an our King."

20. GREAT MISCHIEF

KING OF THE ASHKINS? King! If Arl was struck with dismay, Fith in his delight made up tenfold for his friend's silence. It was the answer to—to everything! If the two branches of the Tiddi came to agree—and why should they not?—they could be one folk again, and instead of King, Fith, Issa's son, would one day be Singer as he had dreamed. It explained, too, why for all their mistrust the Ashkins had taken the three friends in and allowed them to move freely through the Mountain, despite the danger to all that discovery would mean; and why the youngles had abandoned hard-learned caution to follow a stranger's lead.

Amidst the excitement, old Vordibee rose, made a deep, formal bow, and motioned Arl to his side. Indicating that Arl should sit in the stone chair, he sat himself down on the bench at Arl's right and leaned close to whisper in his ear. Arl listened in a daze.

Olders had their daydream-games too, it seemed, though few cared or dared to admit so. Vordibee's, refined and polished over six score years, had, he confessed, been elaborated into a full-fledged plan in which eventualities were allowed for and every miscalculation had its remedy.

When Arl had heard the whole of it, he stood and held up a hand for silence.

"Vordibee the Wise has a plan."

When at last two messengers came to the upper level barracks in search of Koorg the Illigan, they found it emptied of all but a handful of guards. A small patrol of these sent to the Ashkin quarters found all in order: the door locked fast and the guards nodding drowsily beside it, but awake. Nabb? No, they had not seen Nabb. Nor Koorg. No, no trouble from the little folk. The work gangs had returned early to be locked safely away from the Springday ceremonies. No trouble at all.

The trouble was to come. First to smell the smoke were the guards before the entrance to the Dancing Floor. At the orders of the Captain of Gzel, one Rokarrhuk was sent to investigate. He came back from the level below at a stumping run. Fire in the mines! The captain bared his teeth. On this of all afternoons! He sent four of his eight guards to spread the alarm and bring back firefighters, then uncoiled his lash and turned back to the Dance.

At the far end of the long, gently sloping corridor leading off the stone-curtained gallery around the Dancing Floor, a doorway led onto a stair landing. The downward flight led to the level where the Rush, pouring down from above, ran for a way in its old, worn channel and then vanished down the shaft that led toward the Wizards' Way. Not far beyond lay the iron-grated mouth of the mine shaft. Dark, oily smoke filled the passages and nearby storerooms and rolled up the stair in search of open doors (for some had been left open and others as carefully closed).

Thin gray drifts had begun to gather under the kitchens' high, blackened ceilings before the first squadron

172

from the lower level barracks arrived to fill leather buckets and water sacks in the Rush. There was a long delay while a second key to the iron grate was found ("Where *is* Koorg?" the squadron leader roared). Once a line some hundred guards long had descended the smoky shaft and groped through the galleries toward the fire, the water that passed along it seemed, most strangely, to spread the blaze rather than to quench it.

By the time it was discovered that the blaze was an oil fire, it was too late. The oil had been tipped down an airwell from a storeroom above—a storeroom full of fat-bellied storage jars that could be rolled along very handily, six Ashkins to a jar.

The Ashkins watched and waited anxiously in the nearest of the rubble-filled chambers along the dark passage beyond the mine mouth. Arl, when he no longer heard the thud of heavy-booted feet upon the stair, crept out into the shadowed passage to count heads. Only the commander and half a dozen soldiers handing buckets from the Rush's brim to their fellows on the downward ladder were left in the smoky, torchlit chamber. Their hides were tough, Fith had warned, remembering his own encounter with a shiver, and so Arl counted out fourteen sleep-darts. Lying prone, the better to steady his aim, he fixed on the nearest pair of hairy, unprotected knees and let fly.

Buckets sloshed and shoulders drooped, but there could be no waiting for sleep to overtake the swaying soldiers. Thickwitted or no, the Rokarrhuk in the shaft would quickly know something was amiss. The Ashkins did not wait for the darts to finish their work, but swarmed out like a hive of angry bees and rushed the dazed and bellowing Rokarrhuk over the shaft's rim. In quick order the Rokarrhuk were followed down by cartloads of rubble laboriously hauled up that same shaft by the hands that now tipped it down again.

With the shaft filled, a score of eager hands raised the heavy iron-grate hatch to slam it shut. Once locked, it was sealed—its keyhole jammed with a pebble and filled up with quick mortar.

"Come, there's nothing here," Lek urged, with an impatient look around the untidy Star Chamber. "We were too long in finding this place. There is no telling what great mischief the Tiddi are stirring their mountain kin to. We must get them out and away."

"It is not *their* great mischief we need worry about." Ollo's face was grim as he bent over the parchments on the great table. "But you are right. There is nothing here. And everything. The empty crystal case might well have held Twelve Stones. These writings tell the tale I feared, but nothing of him who plots it."

The Wizard straightened. "Clearly this Naghar—wizard or sorcerer, I cannot tell—came to the Opal Mountain for the same reason that you sought it: because here are to be found stones like those the Maker Kyth mined here. Unless I misjudge, he has aimed, through trial and error, to ape the Great Dance and use its power to an end that *he* misjudges, for it can only mean the world's end. It is madness! I pray the stars I may be wrong, but if it is so, many things fall into place. Think of the year's great Dancing Days, and the great storms and earthshakes on the Midwinter Eve past and many another quarterday eve."

Lek, who had paused in his impatient pacing to frown at a shabby, wine-black cloak hanging beside a long, dark gold-framed mirror, gave a start. "And sunset cannot be far off." Without thinking, he drew a hand down the cloak's worn folds and then reached up to slip it from its hook. Settling it around his shoulders, he turned to the mirror and saw—nothing.

"Excellent!" said Ollo. "Such a cloak may prove useful if we must search this Naghar out. He will be the more easily found without it, and we the less. But where are we to look? The strange pillared room below seems made for a Dancing place, but it was deserted." Moving to the mirror, he touched it with his fingertips and muttered two or three soft words Lek could not make out. "Hah, see there!"

As he pointed, the black mirror clouded as if it were a window onto a night fog. Clearing patchily, as a mist clears, it showed a strange forest of rose and green on the shore of a dark lake. A tall, hooded figure robed in midnight blue strode along that shore, followed by two Illigans.

"Of course!" Ollo struck his staff upon the floor, and the mirror's face grew blank. "I am a fool! Come, we have wasted precious time. Where would this mockery of the Great Dance be held but in the hall where Basadil's folk celebrated the Gatherings!"

As they hastened downward along the City's corridors and stairs, only once did Lek and Ollo see any of the Naghar's soldiers, and then it was a lone Rokarrhuk trotting heavily upward on some errand. Once the soldier was safely past, Ollo set a young Man's pace and took the long stairs at so headlong a rush that Lek marveled and thought he must after all be, at least in part, of Silvrin blood. Wizards were longer lived than other Men, even those of kings' blood, his grandmother had said, half-jesting, that her own great age must betray a distant touch of royalty. In Ollo it would have to be more than a touch of Aldarin. Surely no Man living—not even the wisest of the Wise—could remember Basadil's rule in Avel Timrel . . .

and if, by magic or no, he could, such a Man could never match paces with Ollo. Danger seemed to have livened more than the Wizard's wits.

A good league to the south, and many levels lower, they came to the Hall of the Pillars where six ways met, and there encountered Fith and Findral with a troop of forty or fifty Ashkins hurrying out from another passage.

"Quickly!" said Ollo briskly. "Which of these ways leads to Basadil's Great Hall?"

The Ashkins looked alarmed, startled both by the question and the questioner. Lek heard the name Zadil whispered anxiously among them. It was young Gelly who pointed to the wide, worn path polished smooth by miners' feet that led to the second archway beyond the stair curving down along the wall.

Ollo frowned. "What is there in Basadil's name to set you all a-twitter? And," he added, "what has happened that you make your way so foolhardily, chattering and keeping no lookout?"

"What should we look out for?" Fith's eyes danced. "We have not seen a guard all this hour. The North Gate is closed fast. When the day guards paraded out through the ranks of the waiting night guards, two of us pulled the block away from the wheel that winds up the portcullis chain. The grating came down with a dreadful clang and shut them all out. My ears ring still."

Young Gelly's excitement overcame his awe of Men. "They shot through the grating with zpears an arrowguns, but we zhut the great doors on them. Now we go to join Arl the King."

Lek stared, and Ollo's brows shot up. " 'Arl the King'? This is something new! But there is no time to stand and gossip. And go more warily. You may yet find trouble."

So saying, the Wizard drew his cloak once more about

him and vanished down the southerly corridor, with Lek a shadow at his heels.

Coming up the stair out of the kitchens, Arl saw two fleeting shadows pass the stair's head. Meeting Fith and the others as they came along behind, he sent the Ashkins down to hide in the ovens until their friends came up from the mine head below. Then, with Fith and Findral, he hurried in the Wizard's wake. They scarcely saw the beauties of the way they followed, the many-colored walls and crystal-tipped stone icicles that undulated along the ceiling and shone in the torchlight like a river of stars flowing downward, deeper into the mountain.

At the foot of a short flight of stairs the way widened briefly. There the Tiddi came upon a spellbound Ollo leaning over a low, circular wall set in the middle of the passage. As the Tiddi came near, the Wizard thrust out a warning arm. "Take care!" He spoke thickly, and bore a look of deep dismay.

Fith peered over the wall and drew back quickly. Arl and Findral essayed a cautious look and could not turn away. Two hundred feet below, tiny figures moved upon a dark and gleaming floor, a lake not of ice or water, but of glass.

Fith edged closer. "W-where did Lek go?"

The Wizard's dark eyes for a moment looked less bleak, and he gave a glimmer of a smile. "No, young sprat, he has not fallen over. He took one look, said something about a cat, and raced ahead. He does not know what he races to!"

With a swirl of cloak, Ollo too was gone.

"*Cat?*" Together Arl and Fith and Findral leaned out over the parapet once again.

From their vantage point the friends could see only the expanse of floor directly below. As they watched, a procession of tiny figures curved across that gleaming darkness. Two by two they came, all richly robed, some bearing lamps, twelve wearing crowns upon their heads —golden caplets agleam with gems. A thin, clear wail of music, drums and flutes and jangling bells, floated upward.

"I do not see Cat," Fith said. "Where is she? Where is Cat?"

"There," said Findral in his ear. "In front of all the others."

Neither of the Tiddi were as sharp-eyed as Findral the Wolf, but as the head of the procession circled back into sight, there indeed was Cat, larger than the others and moving with a longer, surer stride.

Arl stiffened. "A lamp—Is it a lamp she carries?"

"It winks too brightly," Fith said doubtfully.

Findral drew back to stand with his forepaws on the parapet. His eyes met Arl's. "It is no lamp. It is a stone. A fiery golden stone."

21. THE LORD NAGHAR

Lek slowed his headlong downward race to hesitate a moment where the stair forked. Wisdom counseled waiting for the Wizard, for the City's paths could lead in unexpected directions; but the glimpse of Cat in her golden robes and caplet, with the blinding thing she carried—a flame? a stone?—had filled him with a dread he feared to put a name to.

The right-hand way plunged down more steeply but, as if by instinct, Lek veered to the left down the shadowy wider curve. At the stair's foot the passage sloped gently down. After some fifty yards it opened out and up into a splendid antechamber. Dark crystals on its walls glittered in the faint lamplight from the Great Hall beyond, and at its far end tall, slender columns gathered to support a wide arch that opened out onto a lake of starlit water circled by a still, moon-silvered forest.

As Lek drew closer the illusion faded, and the lake became the wide, dark floor he had seen from above. The trees were pale, branching columns overhung by massive dripstone formations uncannily like thick-clustered leaves. Crystal floor and cunningly carved trees alike gleamed in the light from green crystal lamps strung among the stony branches.

From his shelter among the archway's columns, the conjuror searched for the winding procession of Dancers, but saw no sign of them. Across the floor's dark expanse, lamplight glinted on the bows and spears of soldiers. A small company of Rokarrhuk was drawn up among the mighty tree trunks massed along the further borders of the hall. There, opposite the pillared entrance, the two greatest of the trees met in an arching canopy. In their broad shadow a massive throne stood. A plain, high-backed seat of clear green stone, it stood atop a round, four-stepped dais cut from the same dark crystal or fire-glass that made the floor. On the first step on either side stood Illigans in furred gowns of mingled brown and purple, and in the high seat sat their Lord, a dark figure robed and cloaked in midnight blue, shadowy and half seen.

In the same moment that Lek's gaze touched upon him, the Naghar stiffened and leaned a little forward. Lek drew back out of sight. Something of power and impatience in that ominous posture was disquieting, alarmingly familiar. It was the Naghar's dread shadow he had seen in the Ice Mirror in Gzel as that dark will overmastered his own. But this was something more than dread. . . .

In the green and silver gloom of that vast, high-domed room the face of the Lord of Nagharot was only a pale blur. Come, take heart, Lek told himself. The strangeness of the place was enough to set the palest imagination to spinning fantastic webs. And yet—the lift of a gloved hand, the sweep of a furred sleeve, the arrogant lift to the head. . . .

Lek shivered but then, whispering Ollo's spell *Irsilo nánne silar* twice again for safety's sake, he drew the Naghar's discarded cloak close about him. Striving for the concentration the wizard had demanded of him out on the snowy river of ice, he glanced down and saw as before only the dark, glassy floor. So easy! But without the cloak he could not have done it.

Moving quietly but swiftly, he skirted the columns and made for the sheltering eaves of the arc of trees on his left hand. The shadows there were not deep. Within four yards he met the chamber's curving wall, and this he followed, stepping silently around the hall's rim. Unseen or no, he did not care to fall under the Naghar's eye. He slipped through the deep shadow behind the high seat into the trees beyond and returned to the archway. He had counted thirty soldiers, but the Dancers were vanished.

And where was Ollo? Surely not wandering again in the corridors of his mind. Oh Stars, not at such a time as this!

"Where is Koorg? The time is almost upon us."

Lek saw the Naghar raise his staff and with it strike sparks from the glassy dais as the smooth, angry voice cut through the waiting silence. "Have the messengers gone by way of the Owl Mountains? Koorg should have been here long ago. And you, Griol, what of that tale of a fire? Why have your soldiers not sent one of their number back with news of it?"

The Illigan to his right made a sharp gesture that sent two Rokarrhuk lumbering through the stone trees and out past the watching conjuror. As they went, both Illigans moved around the great circle of hanging lamps, extinguishing all but the dozen or so nearest the high seat. As they finished, the Naghar raised his staff and drew with its tip upon the air pale, spinning images of the nine planets, the Sun and Moon and Wheel-Star. The sorcerer's eyes burned.

"Soon now, soon now! A little while and their powers shall be my powers. Already I have stirred Aalenor's realm in the sea's deeps, and the Four Winds of Haumurel.

Now come the lordship of Aturil and Tionel's strength; all the power of Lis and the darkness that is Azilar . . . all ordered anew with Nirim, the planet of change and death at the center!"

With a wave of his dark-gloved hand, all but the shadow Lis vanished. Of it, only a dwindling shard remained, as if the watchers in the mountain's heart saw the Sun as she slipped below the World's rim.

"Soon. . . ." The Naghar stirred restlessly, as if he woke from a trance or dream. "Where is old Vordibee? I sent for him and that little ratling Nabb." The rich voice, as silky as it had been hard before, purred with an undercurrent of excitement. "No matter. It is too late to send again."

Lek hesitated. Where *were* the Dancers? The Naghar's presence and the dimming of the lights surely meant that here was the Dancing place, and so they must return. But when they did, even though he might snatch Cat away under the stolen cloak, the Dance could still wheel on. With Ollo gone. . . . Drawn by dreadful curiosity and dread of what the Dance could do, he moved to the middle of the floor. As more lamps were darkened, he drew nearer still. The voice, the gloved hands—they drew him too.

The Naghar wore an odd, close-fitting cap of leather the same midnight color as his robes and cloak and like them bordered with fur, but it was set too with gems like tiny, blazing stars. Beneath it, shadowed eyes gleamed under dark, winged brows.

The Naghar laughed softly and spoke as if to himself. "What matter if Koorg or my soldiers are tardy? Only if Basadil and his haughty folk were here for audience could this night to come be sweeter."

As he spoke he turned full-face toward the place where Lek stood rooted; and Lek, seeing the black eyes and thin, crooked nose, staggered as if under a heavy blow.

Azra!

His old master, Azra—the Naghar? Kind Azra? Trickery and cruel betrayal! It was *Azra* then who had stolen the Worldstone. Azra!

Made bold by astonishment and anger, Lek cried out in a loud voice, "Koorg cannot come, nor the Rokarrhuk, for they all are bound in darkness."

The ringing words echoed around the hall's great dome, and as the echoes died away Lek suddenly and with a rush of relief felt Ollo's firm hand upon his shoulder and heard a voice the double of his own cry out, "As *you* shall be, for Nagharot is Avel Timrel once again, and Basadil comes on the morrow."

Lek felt Ollo's unseen staff brush his arm and saw a tiny flame at its tip inscribe images upon the air as the Naghar's had done. As in the Naghar's illusion, instead of Lis the Sun, Nirim the Earthstone rode at the center of things, with great Lis, the Nine, and distant Lurizel circling it like moons. But the center could not hold; Lis with Oniyel and Tionel and all their fellows spun ever more widely and away. Nirim's brilliant blue paled to a silver like Mirelidar's, her Moon's, and both were fixed in darkness—fixed in darkness, it would seem, by the dark will that sought to rule the Dance.

As the illusion faded, Lek's heart sank, for the Naghar threw back his head, as Azra so often had, and gave a great laugh, as one delighted.

"Excellent, Kell! You have added to your skills since we parted. I had not counted on that. Nevertheless, it has taken you longer than I expected for you to find me." He leaned forward, his eyes as surely fixed upon the place where the conjuror stood as if he could clearly see him.

"Welcome at last to Nagharot, my heart's son. You have come in the last nick of time!"

22. TO DANCE THE SUN DOWN

Azra? *Azra!*

Fith, leaning too far out over the parapet, started in alarm and then lurched back wildly to keep from falling. *Heart's son. Nick of time.* What did it mean? Fith hung trembling on the wall's rim, straining to hear more, as Arl came pattering along the passageway.

Arl was breathless. "Bort has been watching the Dancing Floor. The torches are quenched but the guards have not stirred, nor have the Dancers come out. There must be a secret way up to—" He paused, seeing Fith's agitation. "What has happened?"

Fith found his voice at last. "The N-Naghar. He is *Azra!* The Wizard. Lek's old M-Master!"

"Lek's Master! Arl shivered in foreboding and went to peer anxiously over the parapet. "Where is he? Where is Lek?"

"I could not see them, but I heard."

"And Ollo? And the Dancers? What of them?" Because of the parapet's height and the great width of the Hall as it spread out under the high dome, Arl could see nothing more than Fith when he leaned out, though he was taller. He heard a voice raised in challenge and would have listened, but suddenly he cried out and pointed. "Look—there! Lis!"

Directly below, at the floor's center, a small firefly of

light bloomed in the gleaming darkness of the floor itself, blossoming into a brilliant golden disk. In a moment blue Nirim had appeared and dim, silvery Mirelidar, circling the floor's dark sky.

"The sunset! They have the Stones and are dancing the Sun down—dancing below the Great Hall. It's floor must be the ceiling of the Dancing Floor!" He turned and dashed for the stair.

Fith, lingering for a moment, heard the Naghar's deep, silky tones grow more brisk, more reasonable—perhaps dangerously so. *"Yes, for a while I was Azra, when I sought a way to Nirim. Even though the lesser branch of Umeár's Royal House now rules, so that its King came under my sway, his Astronomer held to old cautions and customs. It is a simple matter to seem to die: a potion, a second coffin in the barge that bears one to the City of the Dead. Once you were in the Astronomer's House and Nirim in your hands, Nirim was mine."*

"For you ruled me still."

Even at so great a distance, Fith heard the bitterness in the conjuror's voice. But why did he stand and debate? Did he see nothing? Did the Stones that danced beneath the floor spin their stately circles behind his back?

Nirim! Fith drew a sharp breath. If the Naghar-Azra held the true Nirim, that was why the blue World that spun below glowed so much more vibrantly than the Nine —brighter than any but blazing Lis. *Lisar the Sunstone?* Surely it could not be the true Lisar! Long-lost Lisar . . . Oh stars, not in Cat's hands. . . .

Slowly, as the Dancers wove sunset's brilliant pattern on the midnight floor, its strangeness dawned upon him. They danced the Sun down *backwards!*

Fith sprang away and pelted up the winding passage to the kitchen stair.

. . .

With a great effort Lek mastered his anger. It had already cost him too dearly, for as his guard fell, so had the spell of the sorcerer's cloak. He bowed, fully visible, and wished Ollo had not suddenly abandoned him.

"You may mock me with your welcome, but you do not rule me now, for I too have some wizardry." Grasping the staff Ollo had left in his hand, he drew a rayed star upon the floor and stepped within its protection.

The Naghar frowned, but then, with a glance over Lek's shoulder, seemed to find there some secret amusement. "Wizardry? Poor Kell! I said that 'for a while' I was Azra. But I have been Zim too, and Azzil, and Orrin. I had thought you would follow closer upon Orrin's trail, you see. But now at last, tonight, I am my unmasked self. I am Arrn, King and Sorcerer, and tonight I sit in Basadil's seat, and you shall sit below me on my right hand. When the Dance is finished, the little princess whom the Tiddi call Cat shall come to sit upon my left."

"But why?" Lek whispered. "Why?"

"*Arrn?* The Sorcerer grandson of Tion of Aam?" The hackles rose on Findral the Wolf's back as he made room for Ollo to pass by. "Is it possible?"

"Of course it is possible," snapped Ollo as he threaded his way down through the Ashkins crowded on the narrow stair. "He is more than half Silvrin, and there are mere Men who have lived for half an age. I knew him for Arrn from the moment I saw Lisar the true Sunstone in your friend Cat's hands."

"C-can't you stop him?" Fith hurried, breathless, at the Wizard's heels.

"Hah! My wizardry is child's play to Arrn's power. But if Lek can hold him for a while and pluck at his curiosity, I may have time to do what I can."

In the darkness at the stair's foot Ollo bade the Ashkins make a little space where he might sit down. There, in the crowded darkness, he sat with his eyes closed and rubbed his hands together as if he washed them. Just as Findral began to worry that the old Man had fallen back into confusion, a faint light began to glow between the Wizard's palms. He continued rubbing, and by slow degrees the light grew until it flashed out between his fingers, and his hands seemed a golden lamp with shadowed bones for ribs. When he uncupped them a radiant globe of light blazed out like a second Lisar.

"Now, put it in your pocket," he instructed Fith, "until I have need of it."

Fith obeyed nervously, and to his surprise found the golden fire cool and weightless. It glowed through the pocket of his leather tunic like an orange autumn moon.

Ollo eased open the door into the stone-curtained gallery around the Dancing Floor and found an impatient Arl already waiting there and the shadows full of Ashkins. Whereas before the gallery had glowed with the torchlight that shone through its stone curtains, now the room beyond was dark save for the luminous Stones that danced there. The strange, discordant music wound through the darkness and set the Ashkins to stirring anxiously. The Wizard bent to whisper in Arl's ear.

"Fith carries a little something in his pocket he must slip to Cat in exchange for Lisar. How many guards? We must take them quietly, and the Dance must seem to go on."

"Four now. Two were sent to ask about the fire, and then two more. They did not come back . . ." Arl stopped and stared for a moment in disbelief. "To go *on?*" Reassured by a nod and the gleam in Ollo's eye, he turned to send the first of the Ashkins creeping through the darkness of the gallery toward the guarded opening onto the darkened Dancing Floor itself.

"And where is Cat?" Lek's voice was strong, arrogant even, but the effort it took to keep it so left him shaken. He was glad of Ollo's staff for more reasons than one. Arrn's will beat upon him like a heavy summer's sea upon a sandy shore. The star he drew so confidently upon the floor had, at a wave of Arrn's gloved hand, unravelled itself and now made a braided knot, now a spiraled maze. "Where is she?"

Exultation blazed in Arrn's eyes. "Turn and see! Come stand by me and see where she dances the stars out of their courses!"

Lek wheeled, and for the first time saw the lights that moved beneath the floor. Whirling back, Ollo's staff thrust out before him, he forced his way to the dais' foot step by leaden step.

"So, great Arrn! You hint that we are kin—well, if I have been a bitter fool, then you are power's fool. This Dance you mock is, as the Sky's Circles are, a figure of the whirling balance at the heart of things. Would you see the whole fly apart, destroyed to prove your power? When you and your power must perish with it?"

"No," whispered the Sorcerer. His eyes blazed, and one gloved hand struck the chair's arm. "The mountains may tumble about us, but *here* will be the storm's still eye."

"No, Sorcerer, here!"

As the high, light voice rang out like silver over the star-crossed floor, Arrn surged to his feet in anger and alarm. Lek turned and saw Cat framed in the far archway, clear-eyed and defiant in her golden robes, with Lisar ablaze in her cupped hands. As if in a dream, he saw her take the Sunstone in one hand, draw that hand back and, like a child rolling a ball, send the Star-Stone through the ante-

room and spinning down the outer corridor's long curve.
"*NO!*"

The cry rent the air, and as it died away the Sorcerer's shape loomed up to tower like a midnight shadow among the pale green lamps, a shadow that gathered itself up into a dark whirlwind of sound and sped after the rolling Stone.

Through the door at the corridor's far end it rolled and down a long stair and then another, then beside the Rush's watercourse and past the mine the river drowned. The shaft to the Wizards' Way led downward once again, and in the windowed room above the water stair, the shimmering globe rolled down a new-opened shaft that had been sealed since it had been, for its dangers, abandoned in Basadil's time.

Down gallery and shaft it plunged and down deeper galleries still. At the last, trembling on the edge until Arrn spied it, it tumbled into the wide, bottomless crack at the mountain's root.

And the rushing wind that was Arrn, once King of Aam, shrieked out in rage and followed.

23. NEW CIRCLES

AN HOUR BEFORE DAWN on the morning of Tinnimoon Day, the Tiddi of Avel Timrel cut away the last block of stone from before the East Gate of the City, and The Great Gate which had not opened since Basadil's folk sealed it shut, unfolded at last upon the fading starlight of a clear sky. The Shadow had blown away.

Youngles ran out to caper in the cool air. Their elders hung back until Bort and his brothers came with the good news that there was no sign of the Dread Ones or their riders or the companies of Rokarrhuk that had camped below the North Gate. "They must have fled through their tunnel once they saw the stars and knew the Shadow was fled," Arl said.

Together with Lek and Cat, Findral and Fith, Arl led the mountain folk across the wide Annul valley to the Fennethelen's Inner Gate where, to her awe and delight, it was Cat's hand against the print of Basadil's that opened the great doors. They carried torches with them to light the dark Way, but when they came at the bottom to the Sun Gate's high hall they quenched them all in the Rush.

The tall stone doors needed no magic to be opened from the inner side, and at Arl's touch they swung wide. In the rush of light the mountain Tiddi fell down in wonder, covering their eyes against the golden dawn. Far in the east the rim of Lis lifted over the high Blues and shone down the long glacier that fed the ice river girdling the Fennethelen and gilded it with light. When they dared to peep between their fingers they saw a great marvel.

Down that golden road, with Hlik and the Ravens of Domgrath flying as their heralds, came all the Wolves of Aam.

And Basadil and all the bannered Silvrin host.

The Silvrin sealed the old mine shaft fast with stone and spell and carved deep a verse of warning around the circle of the capstone. Ollo, freed from his vigil, with a sigh let go his spell of Making, leaving the will-o'-the-wisp he had fashioned into the image of the Sunstone to die back into darkness in the bottomless crack at the mountain's root. Weary, but with a light heart, he climbed to the Great Hall. He found it ablaze with lamps and all the four folk gathered there: the Ravens in the great stone trees above Basadil's seat, the Wolves of Aam before it, and Tiddi and Silvrin mingled on the gleaming floor. Such a company had not met together in all the long years since the Falling of the Seas.

"Ah, here is the Keeper of Aabla. Come, Ollo!"

The Silvrin King beckoned the Wizard to a seat on the step below his own, and as Ollo settled himself, the elf King looked out across the sea of faces.

"The World is older by half an age and more since last I sat here, yet to see this company, it might have been yestereve," Basadil said with grave courtesy. "Indeed, there must be tales enough among us to fill a thousand nights, but for curiosity I must hear their ending first. To the north we met a fleeing army—or the remnant of one—and slew many Dread Ones. Those soldiers who did not wish to fight made for the Owl Mountains and we let them go, for Hlik said we were needed here. Yet the delay has brought us here too late to meet an ancient enemy, I am told. How came he here when the ways were closed against him? And you? And *why*?"

In answer, the folk assembled in the Hall parted a way among them for Lek and Cat, Arl and Findral and Fith. When they stood before the dais, Cat came forward shyly and climbed the four high steps, Lisar the Sunstone held bravely in her bare hands, for its fiery brilliance slept. Basadil took it with a look of wonder, and all the Silvrin, marveling, whispered among themselves. To the Tiddi the sound was like the quiet rustling of silverwillow leaves.

When Lek stepped forward bearing Nirim, the rustle stilled. "After all I have seen," he said, "I think it better that Nirim the Worldstone too should return to Thamor, the land of the Aldar beyond the North. In Umeár I might trade it for my good name, but there it would be no more than a king's bauble, and a dangerous one. I have not lost fourteen years for that."

Third came Findral, bearing in his mouth the Moonstone Mirelidar, brought from its hiding place on the Deep Ice by the Wolves of Aam; and after Findral, Arl. He wore the golden cap of leaves that had been his grandfather Haag's and climbed up to place in Basadil's hand Lek's small shard of red stone.

"By the stars!" Basadil exclaimed. "Here is an unexpected treasure! I saw it last in this very Hall when last I sat here. Tonight we must hear the tale of its adventures, and yours. For now, Arl of the Mountain, I accept it and offer this"—he held out a key with a curious star-shaped shank—"in thanks for keeping Mirelidar safe from Arrn. When the Mountain no longer has a wizard at hand to bind and loose the Rush and the mountain's other waters, you may use this—if your eyes are sharp enough to find the waterlocks."

"But—" Arl looked up in dismay at the King of the Silvrin in his grass-green robes. "You have not come to stay?"

"No, alas, even though in time the restoration of Nirim and the Sunstone will mean the return of summer to these northlands. We left our fastness beyond the Dragon's Teeth and had set out on the long trek east to the Sea and Thamor and beyond when Hlik found us. There are too many Men abroad in Astarlind, and will be more, so we go to join our kin. You shall be King Under the Mountain, not I; and perhaps in time the two Tiddi peoples will share their different Ways. It would do Old Nar good to see new wonders!"

"You know Old Nar?" Fith burst out, amazed.

Basadil laughed. "Yes—and no. We know more of all of you, Issa's son, than you might dream. It is forgotten among the Tiddi, but in Aam oftentimes our folk were mingled, and of the mingling were born the Men of Aam, who were different from the Astarlings and other Men, left-handy and longer lived. Teela, Tion's queen, was more than half a Tiddi."

Arl and Fith exchanged startled glances, and with the Tiddi of the Mountain glanced sidelong in wonder at wide-eyed Cat as the Silvrin King beckoned her forward and Lek after her.

He looked at them a long while before he spoke. "Ardin and Arda. How like them you are, Kell and Kirri of Umeár! It seems no more than a year and a day ago that two young folk who fled Arrn's madness before Aam's fall stood where you stand now. They were my grandchildren, for my daughter Annel was Teran's queen, and Arrn, alas, was her son. Arrn's son Ardin bore a hand scarred like his father's—after the Theft, the Sunstone's mark was on all that line. His elder sister Arda was more Tiddish and more beautiful than all the daughters of Men."

Cat paled. "Then that is why he called me 'granddaughter?' "

"And me 'heart's son,' " said Lek bitterly.

"And so may I call you," chided Basadil. "But you are yourselves nevertheless. And so were Ardin and Arda. At the war's end our kindred saw them safe to Umeár. After that, in Brodinan in the West we heard little news of them and Umeár, only that in the end they went their separate ways—Ardin's children into the green hills of Gallary with their music and magic, and Arda into the King's House as queen."

Lek spoke as in a dream. "It was to steal Nirim that Arrn came as Azra to Umeár, but we fell into his hands like star gifts, to love and hate. I remember . . ." He turned wonderingly to Cat and took her hand. "When I was nine I went with Azra to King Darad's house in Kimmer to see the fairs and fireworks at the birth of the King's firstborn, named Kirri. Kirri! I saw you then!—a tiny babe held up at a castle window to greet the crowds. None ever saw her nearer. A three-month later she died of the summer fever. So Darad said, but he is not a King to scruple at banishment or murder. I can hear him now: 'A darkling child with pointed ears, wife? There is something worse here than your drop or two of cursed Aldarin blood. Away with it!' "

"Perhaps," said Ollo unexpectedly, "but the counsel would have been Azra's—or Arrn's, as it seems we must name him. Fith heard him say as much to Cat."

"Circles within circles," Basadil said softly. "And now, my Children of the Three Folk, you may tread your own paths. Will they lead back to Umeár?"

"No!" said Cat swiftly. "I think I would care for it no more than it would care for me, and all my friends are here."

"No," said Lek more slowly. He spoke in dawning wonder. "I think I care no more for it than it has cared for me. And all my friends are here."

Fith and Cat and Arl sat in the sunshine by the East Gate, backs to the Opal Mountain, brown legs stretched out, and toes curling and uncurling for sheer pleasure in the warmth. They watched Findral and his brother Forga playing at tag with their young brother Furn. The Silvrin and the greater part of the Wolves were gone, but Renga and Rovanng and their young had stayed to journey west with Cat and Fith to Min, the stopping place beyond Saan on the Tiddi Wandering Way.

Arl sighed. "I wish I were going with you. What am I to do here? Tootoo knows as much of kingship as I do."

At the sound of her name the little owl opened one eye, but closed it quickly against the Sun's glare, shifted a little on her perch atop Fith's tight curls, and went back to dreaming of a dusk full of mice and shadows.

Fith drew up his knees and wrapped his arms about them. "I wish too. But—" He brightened. "You will not be rid of us for long. Not even a dozen Old Nars could keep Issa and Singer and Starwise away. 'A new way to Eem,' Issa will say."

Arl laughed. " 'Lobb's First Way,' Singer will name it."

"Starwise will pick among her stones and see the stars command it," said Cat solemnly, but her eyes danced. "And you need not slide anxious looks at me, friend Arl. I know that when they hear my tale the olders may grumble and wish me gone, but when have they not?"

"But—you are rightful queen in Umeár, they say!"

She grinned. "Umeár would take one look and push me out to sea again."

"Stay here. In Avel Timrel," Arl said suddenly, and found himself holding his breath.

Cat closed her eyes and tilted her face to the Sun. "No.

I have dreams too, Arl-the-Dreamer. I have a dream place. It may be only a wishing dream and not a fore-knowing, but I do not think so. As we came north along the Blues, I dreamed one night that we passed my dream place that very day, but could not see it for the trees: a tall mountain—once a fire mountain, by its shape—tucked between the ridges. Up top, there is a wide, round valley tilted like a cup to catch the Sun. A place to make an end to wandering. Liloes grow there, and persimmons and . . . and, oh, any seed that touches the ground!"

"And you all alone there?" Fith was as astonished as Arl. They had never before heard so many words in a row from Cat. For the first time they felt the depth of her strangeness and realized, with a great sadness, that she truly was not one of them and never would be.

"Alone? Oh, no." Cat's eyes flew open. "I may not be a Tiddi, but I could not bear to be alone."

An odd note to her protest, and the flush that rose with it to her cheeks, brought sharp, puzzled looks from both of her friends, and Cat leaped up as if the sound of foot-steps echoing across the gateway hall came as a welcome interruption. *"Lek! It is Lek she cares for!"* thought Arl and Fith in the same moment, and they stared at each other in amazement and delight.

"It is time to go," Ollo announced briskly as he emerged into the sunshine with Lek and Renga and Rovanng. "We shall journey together awhile, for the speediest way to Min is past Aabla and down the Shining River to Aalen, then cross-country."

"And Lek? Where do you go?" Arl asked.

"To Aabla. For a while," Lek answered. His manner was as cool as ever, but Arl could tell that he was pleased.

"Kell is a trifle old for an apprentice," Ollo said, laugh-ing, "but I have agreed to take him on for a year or three. He has as much to learn of simple magic as of the deeper

New Circles

arts: the secret names and ways of all the beasts and
growing things of Astarlind, the languages of beast and
Manling, Rokarrhuk and Iceling—and of his own heart.
And yes, young Fith, of levitations and transformations
and other skills that astonish and amaze! We mean to
return here for Midsummer Feast Day, and you shall
judge how he fares. But now come, take up your packs!"

Together they crossed to the Inner Gate and went down
the long road through the Fennethelen to the Sun's Gate.
There Arl bade the travelers farewell. He watched as Lek
and the Wizard took Cat and Fith upon their shoulders
for the difficult westward trek along the ice river, for its
surface had become deep slush and a tangle of shallow
meltwater streams.

Arl watched until the nine small figures were lost in the
dazzle of afternoon sun upon the watery ice, and then
turned back toward the open Sun's Gate.

There, sitting on the threshold, was Snip.

"Snippet!" Arl was startled. "You have come all this way
after us, and then did not bid our friends farewell?"

Snip shrugged. "I vollow you, not them. Gelly zaid you
druther go way with your vriends. I was avraid. Zo I
come, to be zure."

"And you have had no noonmeal on your way?" Arl
smiled and bowed, with his hand to his forehead in the
manner of one of the ancient Tiddi greetings, and said to
the dark-eyed child, "I am honored indeed. Had I known
of your coming, I would have prepared a feast. Instead—"
He pulled from his pocket half of a nutcake, the remnant
of his own noonmeal and the last of the supply he had
brought from Saan in his carrying sack.

When Snip had devoured the cake, she cocked her head
and frowned. "What is a veast?"

"What is a *feast?*" Arl was astonished but then realized

that, of course, the mountain folk could not know. They were Tiddi, and had never feasted!

"Come!" he said suddenly. He snatched up Snip's small hand in his own and pulled her after him. "We have plans to make and work to do! There is the Wolf Way to be mended. Tables to be made. And wagons, to send south for nuts and fruit and grains. Seeds to be sent for, and gardens planted . . . and only three moons until Midsummer Feast!"

They ran.